The Manner of Amy's Death

Carol Mackrodt

For William

"Fiction is the lie through which we tell the truth."

Albert Camus

Prologue

September 1560 - Farewell, Cumnor Place

The worst thing when someone dies, after the shock of knowing that you'll never again talk to them or laugh with them, share their sorrow or have good times, is the terrible moment when you have to sort through their possessions, those sad and cherished souvenirs of a life now over, those little things of no value that once gave them so much pleasure. I'm sad, oh yes, so sad for my friend and I'm furious.

Where's her husband in heaven's name? He should be doing this, not me.

But as usual he's occupied elsewhere so, as Amy's lifelong friend, this miserable task has fallen to me. It's now nearly three weeks since she died, just twenty eight years old, and I still can't quite believe it. The two wooden chests that have been our faithful companions on our endless travels from Lincolnshire to Kent, from Essex to London and from London to Oxfordshire stand open, half filled with Amy's gowns, kirtles, hoods and velvet embroidered slippers once again – as if we're making just another journey. She'd always wanted a home of her own with her beloved Robert but it didn't happen.

Sir Robert Dudley! – I say the words with disgust and contempt. Where have you been all these years? She trusted you and waited for you to come home, waited for affectionate little notes that never arrived? And where were you when she died, Dudley? Oh yes I know very well … walking with your lady love, laughing and giggling with her, and your wife conveniently far away where you could forget about her – as you have for the past two years. Why would I have thought you'd have any difficulty with that? I hate you. And I hate your lady friend even if she is the Queen.

As I look around her chamber strewn with fine clothes and cherished possessions, it seems as if Amy and I are simply preparing for yet another move to yet another manor house where we'll be treated as privileged guests.

It's not the case – and never will be again. She's dead; my lovely friend is gone forever. She's lying in a cold vault in the Church of Mary the Virgin in nearby Oxford, all alone and asleep in the dark. She hated the dark. What was the prayer we would say at night when we were small? "Matthew, Mark, Luke and John, bless the bed that I lie on." I sit down on the edge of the bed and think of Amy in her cold bed, the tears rolling down my face.

There are footsteps on the stairs outside, the heavy measured tread of a man. I dry my tears and try to look less emotional as Sir Anthony Forster enters the chamber. He was Amy's host during her last months, a favour to his friend, Sir Robert. But Cumnor is not his; the manor house is rented from a doctor called Mr Owens.

"Are you making good progress, Katherine?" He then sees my tear stained face. "It's a terrible task I know. Why not take some time in the Hall with the rest of us and enjoy a cup of ale and a sweet cake."

"Thank you for your kindness, Sir Anthony, but I'd rather finish. Robert – I suppose I should say *Sir* Robert now - has said that he wants very few of the personal items that belonged to Amy so ….."

"Not even a keepsake?" Mr Forster is incredulous.

"Well, he's asked for the large jewels and her brooch, the Dudley one she wore when her portrait was painted ...... so I asked her brother, John, if her sisters would like her dresses, hoods and slippers. I'm packing them in the chests that .... served us well on our travels." At this point I have to choke back the tears again as I remember how Amy loved fine clothes. Robert, on her death, had immediately demanded all items of high value, precious stones and gold, to be returned to him - but nothing of true sentimental value. He wants no reminders of his marriage. There's a silence. I wonder who will get her jewels – I *know* who.

When I've composed myself, Sir Anthony says, "What about you Katherine – is there nothing you would like?"

"I couldn't wear her clothes. They would remind me too much of her and she always felt she was, well, very grand and beautiful when she wore them even though Robert treated her carelessly and caused her to feel she was worthless."

I've embarrassed poor Sir Anthony by speaking so freely and thoughtlessly. Robert Dudley is a friend of his. He pauses and then, to my surprise, he says, "We will all have to answer to God one day, Kate." It's almost, but not quite, a criticism of Robert who, though shocked at Amy's death, has not been near Cumnor Place for the fifteen months we've been here - not even when he heard of the tragedy. No wonder poor Amy died broken hearted and in despair. Nor did he attend his wife's funeral, a grand affair that cost him a small fortune. Why the expense? Remorse? A guilty conscience? I just wonder.

Sir Anthony takes a key from the top of an oak table and unlocks the drawer underneath. He lifts out a small wooden casket and a bundle of letters tied with ribbon. "The letters were not valuable to anyone but Amy. They are probably from Robert. Will you take them and look after them, Katherine? Someone should do so."

"I'd be pleased to have them. Thank you."

There's another key in the drawer. He unlocks the casket, which Robert's manservant must have missed when he came to collect Amy's diamond and other gems; it contains some small pieces of jewellery from the early years of the marriage - not many as Robert had little money to spare at that time. Later he was attainted, a penniless traitor imprisoned in the Tower while the loving Amy stood by him. These were bad times and, for many years, the young couple had nothing to live by and depended on the charity of their families and friends.

Upon his release Robert and his brothers spent huge sums of money fighting Prince Philip's wars and still Amy waited patiently for better fortune which, for her, never arrived. As Robert's star rose again Amy was slowly and surely cast aside. He spent money gambling at cards or placing wagers on jousts or tennis matches and, yes, he started buying presents too, very expensive presents - but not for her. By this time there was another woman in Robert's life and her name was Elizabeth, the same Elizabeth who is now our Queen. The gossip was rife and, while Amy was delighted with the small gifts her husband sent her, it was rumoured that he spent tenfold on lavish gifts for the Queen.

My bitter reminiscences are interrupted by Sir Anthony who has been examining the contents of the casket.

"Here, Kate, you must take this. It's the necklace she wore, she once told me, when her portrait was painted for her wedding. I'm sure you would like it."

"But what about her sisters, Anne and Frances, or the wives of John and Philip?" Amy has two half sisters and two half brothers, all from her mother's first marriage to Roger Appleyard.

"And you are her family too. She would have wanted you to have this and I know she valued it because she wore it often."

I hold the necklace in the palm of my hand and look at the miniature portrait on the table, her wedding portrait. A fair haired girl of eighteen looks out into the distance with an honest, steady gaze. Amy was a beauty when this portrait was painted just before their grand wedding at the royal palace of Sheen and there's the necklace her father gave her and, on her gown, the Dudley brooch, framed with oak leaves and gillyflowers, worn with pride and love. It had been a gift from Robert but he's now obviously forgotten its meaning. The Latin words for oak, quercus robur, meant 'Robert the oak' to Amy – it was a joke. The gillyflowers represented eternal love, which, I reflect bitterly, was another joke.

The necklace sits warmly in my palm and I feel the rush of love that Amy always invoked with her lively, kindly personality. I can feel her smiling at me and saying, "Go on, Kat Brereton, my good gossip, take it. I want you to."

9

"It's, it's beautiful. Yes I would love to have it."
I'm too full to say more.

Sir Anthony smiles, "Well that's settled then. I'll
send Mrs Picto to help you otherwise she'll spend all
afternoon chattering to Mrs Odingsells! These
women! They do nothing but gossip!"

That makes me smile anyway. A few minutes
pass by and from the stairs I hear the slow laboured
step of Mrs Picto, who was Amy's personal maid.

"Those stairs will be the death of me," gasps the
rather plump lady. She then blushes as she realises
what she's just said. Amy's body was found at the
foot of a pair of stairs, two short flights with a landing
between them.

"Never mind, Mrs Picto, you're here now. You
can help me sort through the last of Lady Dudley's
possessions."

We work through the next hour, placing in four
heaps small items - from the casket a pearl brooch, a
gift from her father, from the drawer two velvet
French hoods decorated with pearls, an embroidered
purse made of velvet, a dried orange studded with
cloves, a prayer book, a decorated mirror, five pairs
of dainty gloves, some handkerchiefs and ribbons, a
pair of red leather riding gloves to match the
embossed leather saddle Robert gave her soon after
their wedding when she was still learning to ride, like
a lady of the royal court.

Her closest living female relatives are Frances and
Anne, her two half sisters, and the wives of her half
brothers, John and Philip Appleyard. We'll leave any
further distribution to the cousins to them. She has
another half brother, Arthur, the illegitimate son of
her father, Sir John Robsart. He and John Appleyard

10

will have to negotiate with Robert Dudley for the lands her father left to his only legitimate child.

Mrs Picto finds a miniature of Robert Dudley, painted when his father was Duke of Northumberland early in 1553, when Robert was nineteen years old.

"He was handsome, wasn't he?" says Picto.

"He still is if you like a swarthy gypsy look," I say. I feel full of contempt for the man who let my dear friend down so badly.

"Do you think he'll want this likeness back?" says Picto.

"What, so he can give it to his new lady love, the Queen?"

"Hush, Miss Katherine," says Mrs Picto looking round fearfully. "The walls have ears, you know."

Well I really don't care any longer but I change the subject.

"Have you been questioned yet by the coroner's jury?" I ask.

"Well I spoke to Mr Smythe, the foreman of the jury, the other day."

"And what did he ask you, Mrs Picto?"

"He wanted to know why Lady Amy had been behaving so strangely on the day she died."

"And what did you say to that?"

"I told him what I said to Mr Blount."

"Which was?"

"Why, how she had been very angry with us and how she had insisted that we all went to the fair in Abingdon so she could be left alone at Cumnor Place - and how old Mrs Owen and Mrs Odingsells refused to go because it was the Lord's Day and no time to be going to a fair. And how there was an argument and how Lady Amy had screamed at them but they still

11

wouldn't go. And how we had to leave her like that and how the next time we saw her she was dead."

"Is that all?" Mrs Picto does not notice the note of irony in my voice. She just can't help gossiping to people.

"No, that isn't all - for he asked me if she was often in a strange mind like that. And I said that indeed I had often heard her praying to God to be delivered from her suffering. And then I was amazed. He asked me if I thought she had an evil toy in her mind. 'Good sir,' I said shocked, 'My Lady Amy was a good girl and loved God and said her prayers like a good Christian woman. I'm sorry I said so much if you think I was meaning that she took her own life.' "

I look skywards to heaven. Oh, Mrs Picto, if only you thought before using your tongue. Fortunately the jury must have come to the conclusion that Amy's death was accidental for she'd been given a Christian burial. On the basis of Picto's foolish ramblings they could well have reached the conclusion that Amy, in a fit of desperation and dejection, had tried to kill herself by flinging herself down the stairs, a most evil act for which the dead person would be buried at a crossroads with a stake driven through the heart to prevent their wicked spirit from wandering and tormenting others.

"This little needlework case is nice," says Mrs Picto.

"Yes it was a present from her husband last Christmas."

"Well that was nice of him."

"Yes, except I heard he'd presented the Queen with gemstones and two pairs of her favourite silk stockings."

"What! Silk stockings all the way from Spain? They must have cost a fortune."

"Apparently, they did."

"Well that was a kind thing to do too. I expect, being a Queen, her legs are more delicate than ours."

"Hm. The stockings were black. I always think that a man who gives a woman a pair of black stockings cannot wait to see what they look like when she wears them."

"Miss Katherine!" says Mrs Picto in a shocked voice. Then we both laugh.

"Well Mrs Picto, no man will ever see my stockings, black or white. I intend never to marry for I think no one will ask me!" We laugh guiltily. Laughter seems so out of place here.

By this time we've almost finished clearing the chamber. I'm busy writing labels while seated at the table, 'a pearl brooch for Arthur Robsart's wife', and so on, while Mrs Picto attaches the labels with ribbons to the items in question and places them carefully in the travelling trunks. A servant has been sent by Sir Anthony with some refreshments since we won't join them in the Great Hall next door.

"So now there's only the miniature portrait of Amy on the table, the miniature of Robert, and Amy's sewing things to assign," I say.

"Maybe Sir Anthony would like the miniature of Sir Robert," says Picto.

"No, I asked him. He said he doesn't wish to own it." That speaks volumes to me. Sir Anthony is known locally as a very honest and respectable gentleman.

"Maybe Mr and Mrs Hyde of Throcking would like it," I continue, "They're Sir Robert's very good friends and have been most generous towards us all in the past."

So the label goes on the miniature, 'For Mr Hyde of Throcking'

"And I think John Appleyard should have his sister's wedding portrait."

"That only leaves Lady Amy's needlework," says Picto.

There's a needlework box containing silk embroidery thread, woollen yarn, needles and a dainty pair of scissors in a case. There are also the remains of a roll of blue sewing silk and a little sewing apron with deep pockets.

"Would you like these, Mrs Picto?"

"Oh, Miss Katherine, I don't know what to say. Maybe they should belong to a lady such as Mrs Odingsells not a humble lady's maid like me."

"Nonsense. You're as fine a needlewoman as anyone I know and, besides, you loved your Lady Amy like a daughter. You looked after her for many years. Amy would want you to have these."

Mrs Picto is overcome by this unexpected windfall. She tries on the apron and places her hands in the pockets, pulling out some threads of silk and a small scrap of paper.

"What's this?"

She opens the paper on which a note has been written but, not being able to read, hands it to me. As I scan the note the hair on the back of my head prickles. It seems to be a note from Robert, a very recent note from Robert.

"To my dearest lady wife, my greetings. I hope that your health is much improved. I am currently at Windsor and intend to make a trip to Compton Verney so that I may search for a manor in Warwickshire. I know that you have long wished for us to have a property that we may call home. I will call at Cumnor on the afternoon of the fair in Abingdon so that we may discuss this further. Please take care that our meeting is in private and send all those of your own kind and your servants to the fair.

Your loving husband, R.D."

I read the note twice just to make sure that this is really happening and the blood drains from my face as I do so. My brain is racing with a myriad of possibilities.

"What is it?" says Mrs Picto. "What does it say?"

"It's er, it's nothing," my voice is a whisper. "Just his last note to her."

"Maybe we should give it to Mr Smythe and the jury," says Picto.

"No, no. It's nothing. I'll put it with the other notes. Don't mention it, it's not important."

What makes me tell such a lie? I'm not normally untruthful. But I am very, very frightened. Everything's coming together and making sense, all the strange events of the past eighteen months. And this explains Amy's desire to be alone in Cumnor Place on the day of her death. Was she expecting her beloved husband to pay her a long overdue visit? Could it be that Amy's death was not an accident after all?

John Appleyard walks into the chamber. I'm in such a state of shock that I don't even hear him on the stair.

"Oh, Mr Appleyard," says Mrs Picto, "You are just in time. We have this minute finished our work."

Amy's brother looks down into the wooden chests and sees all the objects, neatly labelled, on top of the gowns, bodices and kirtles. "Thank you for your thoughtfulness, Katherine, and for your help, Mrs Picto. You have spared me the eternal recriminations of the women in our family and the disputes over who should have had which trinket." He smiles sadly; he knows human nature. "Now let us all go down to a well earned supper."

"You two go down first," I say, "And I will follow presently. I will never again enter this chamber and I wish to say goodbye in private." I lock the two chests and hand the keys to John.

When they're gone I open the note again with trembling fingers and take it to the window. The light is fading fast now.

I read it again and again and my heart beats faster. Dirty work has been done and apparently by Robert Dudley. Why did Amy not destroy the note? Did she too suspect a plot? It would not have been the first time she had suffered such fears.

Ought I to hand the note to the foreman of the jury as Picto suggested? I am very, very afraid. The people involved are influential, powerful people at the top of the royal court and I don't wish to end up at the foot of a flight of stairs with a broken neck like Amy. Further, the well respected Sir Anthony Forster will not thank me for stirring up a scandal so close to home.

What should I do?

I look through the note once more and place it with the other notes in the bundle tied with ribbons. Then I have a thought. I don't know why but I check the writing of this note and another one from Robert written some two years earlier. The writing's not the same. The capital A's for instance are formed in a different fashion and the R.D. is but a poor imitation. Robert's handwriting is more educated, more artistic. Did Amy see this and suspect a plot? Or was she so desperate to see Robert again that she paid no heed?

Worse and worse. Who would have wanted her dead? Robert? The Queen? It's true he was careless with her affections, cruel even, but was he so cruel that he killed her? And Amy, why didn't she notice that it was not his handwriting? Or had she believed it was written by a secretary? There are so many unanswered questions.

Mrs Picto's voice calls up the stairs, "Miss Katherine, everyone is in the Hall waiting for you to come down to supper. Are you quite well?"

"Yes, yes, quite well." Looking down there's a crack in the floor where two boards do not meet firmly. I crush the note in my hand and push it down the crack. "Coming."

Chapter One
Seven Years Earlier - Somerset House, London

I'm fast asleep when the noise wakes me up with a jolt. What in heaven's name is going on! Then I'm aware that there's an argument of monumental proportions going on in the chamber next to mine. My friend Amy and her husband, Lord Robert, are having another quarrel and everyone in this enormous palace must be aware of it. No, I'm wrong! Everyone in England and neighbouring France must be aware of it. The subject of the heated discussion is the usual one – the Lady Elizabeth Tudor, second in line to the throne of England.

Amy and I live in the sumptuous, newly-built Somerset House where her husband, Robert Dudley, is the keeper. Unfortunately Amy's arch enemy, Elizabeth, is the new owner – not that we see much of her as she spends most of her time at Hatfield House or at court with her half brother, the young King Edward. In my beautiful sweet-smelling bedchamber next door to theirs I can't help hearing their shouted conversation through the wood-panelled walls.

"I've said I'm sorry, Amy, but we would not be where we are today if I did not hold such high office and work so hard."

"Work so hard for *her*, you mean!"

"If you are referring to the Lady Elizabeth, I work hard for *her* to provide *you* with the beautiful gowns you so like to wear."

"And while you work so hard, that bastard daughter of the whore Ann Boleyn can flirt with you just as her mother once did with King Henry."

"Amy," says Robert in a shocked voice, "I advise you to curb your tongue. Women have been burned for saying less. Elizabeth may one day be Queen and you would be well advised to remember that and our position."

"Well, if you think what *Oi* say is bad, you should 'ear what the common people call 'er after that affair with King Edward's uncle, Sudeley." Amy speaks in a quieter voice now but, forgetfully, slips back into her Norfolk accent.

"I would remind you that you are not a 'common person' so please do not speak like one, Amy, and you should not be discussing such things with servants. And anyway Thomas Seymour, the Earl of Sudeley, behaved disgracefully while Elizabeth was staying at his house *and* she was only fourteen years old at the time. She was his ward. He was supposed to be taking care of her."

"Oh Sudeley took care of her all right!" spits Amy, correcting her grammar, "His wife knew it too. And your Elizabeth allowed him to walk into her chamber half naked **and** romp with her on the bed. Some say she had his child."

"No she did not."

"How do you know?"

"She told me so herself."

"Oh, so you *are* close then!"

"Amy, I'm losing my patience with you," yells Robert again. There's a silence.

"Listen to me," he continues more quietly and in a reasoning tone, "I'm not defending Elizabeth ...." He's obviously seen the look on her face. "Oh no, I'm not. But she *does* now own Somerset House and we live here because I'm the keeper of the house on her behalf. Nothing more. It's what I do, Amy. It's my position and if I have to talk to the owner from time to time, so be it."

"I know but I don't like her."

"I know you don't but the affair with Sudeley is over and done with and she certainly learned her lesson the hard way. Elizabeth won't behave like that again."

"So you accept that her behaviour was not exactly exemplary," says Amy in a triumphant tone.

"She was foolish. She found herself involved with a traitor and was very fortunate that they couldn't prove that she was plotting the King's overthrow with him. Sudeley went to the block; Elizabeth didn't. You know the evidence."

"She's dangerous, Robert."

"Well it doesn't matter now. She won't be significant for much longer if father's plans work out - nor will the Lady Mary." Robert's voice drops.

"But King Edward is very ill and Elizabeth and Mary are his successors. They are his half sisters. If neither of the two, Elizabeth or Mary, are to succeed to the throne what will happen when he dies?"

"Hush! Keep your voice low. Such talk can be construed as treason," whispers Lord Robert. "I can't tell you everything yet but today I was with father discussing his plans."

"So you didn't ride to Hatfield last night to see Elizabeth?"

"No and I'm sorry, Amy, that we did not get to Ely House today for the strawberry fair as I promised. There are now more important matters afoot."

In the privacy of my chamber I'm wondering what he can mean. One thing is very certain; Northumberland, his father, is up to something.

Well at least Robert's explanation for his whereabouts last night should satisfy Amy. You should have heard the way she was carrying on when he didn't come home. He'd promised Amy that we'd go with a group of friends to his father's home at Ely House where there was to have been a strawberry fair today. Ely has the best strawberries in the whole of England so little wonder Amy had been so looking forward to it but Lord Robert didn't return until this evening. Hence the argument! She'd been furious and full of suspicious thoughts.

"Maybe we can go to Ely House tomorrow," says Amy hopefully. Poor Amy. She sees so little of Robert because of his duties at court that she seizes any opportunity to have him to herself.

"I'm afraid we can't do that, my love. Father requires us all to be at Syon Place tomorrow."

"*Syon!*" screeches Amy incredulously as the argument ignites once more.

Across the panelling, I'm cringing. She hates Syon Place, whatever the urgent business the Duke of Northumberland is plotting, and it's a poor substitute for a day's strawberry picking at Ely House!

"Amy, I'm sorry but there's no choice in the matter. You will go."

"I most certainly **will not** go," says Amy in her high-horse strident tone.

"I don't understand what you have against Syon Place," says Robert's equally loud voice. "It's exactly like Somerset House, built in the same style, modern and fashionable. Most women at court would

21

envy you the choice of two beautiful houses, not to mention our other mansions, Ely House and Durham Place."

It's true. We live in the best palaces in all England. Not bad for two country girls from a manor in Norfolk! Robert's family, the Dudleys, are very wealthy and all powerful and some say Robert's father, John Dudley, Duke of Northumberland and Lord President of the Privy Council, is the most influential man in all England. He advises the young fifteen year old King, Edward, and the King listens to him and, more often than not, does his bidding.

Somerset House, where we now live, was built a few years earlier by the Lord Protector, the Duke of Somerset and King Edward's uncle and first adviser. He was, at the time, even wealthier than the Duke of Northumberland but Northumberland was ambitious, pushed him aside and helped to arrange his downfall. Now poor King Edward, who is only fifteen and whose health is poor, has seen both his uncles, first Sudeley, after the Elizabeth affair, and then Somerset, executed for treason on trumped up charges, and only has Northumberland and his family and friends to depend upon. Edward had loved his uncles, his mother Jane Seymour's brothers, and was devastated by their downfall - so distraught that he had his pet hawk tortured to death to show his advisers how raw his feelings were. It was not a pretty sight by all accounts.

Many people hate Robert's father, John Dudley, Duke of Northumberland. The Duke of Somerset had been well liked and it was rumoured that his trial and execution had been on false charges. And then again there are others who simply resent the influence and ambition of the Dudleys. We do not belong to a popular family!

Somerset House, on the banks of the river, was designed in the Italian style with beautiful tall windows and wide corridors exactly like Somerset's other newly built property, Syon Place, which is nine miles out of London in Richmond. Unfortunately Somerset did not live to enjoy either of his two palatial houses. He was beheaded last year ...... and Robert's father, Northumberland, was chief of the plotters of this extravagant man's downfall.

On Somerset's death, the Duke of Northumberland became the most important person in the land and had possession of Somerset's houses in addition to property of his own. But even this was not enough. Inflamed by his own position and soaring ambition, he forced the Lady Elizabeth to exchange with him her even more magnificent palace, Durham Place, for Somerset House. Elizabeth was furious at the time but Northumberland was even more powerful than she, Henry VIII's daughter, so she had to agree. How Amy did laugh!

Until, that is, Amy discovered that Elizabeth wanted Robert as the keeper of her new London home and that this would demand frequent communications between herself and Robert at Hatfield, Elizabeth's 'home in the country'!

Amy and her rich and handsome husband have been living here for the past six months and I am here with them, Kate Brereton, a gentlewoman companion, best friend and confidant, to the Lady Amy. For a young woman not yet twenty two, Amy's going up in the world; her stars have been in the ascendant since her marriage to Robert three years ago and now she has fortune beyond her wildest dreams. Four years earlier, this pretty country girl with a Norfolk accent, daughter of a wealthy landowner and Lord of the Manor in the Norfolk countryside, had no such expectations and we little thought we would one day live in a noble family that attracted envy, fame – and fear.

My thoughts are interrupted by Amy's shrill voice.

"I just don't like it at Syon. It makes me feel uncomfortable and it has a bad atmosphere. It seems to bring ill fortune to everyone who's there."

I know what Amy means. We've often discussed it. It's not just the fact that Northumberland 'inherited' it when poor Somerset went to the block. Syon House was built on the site of a monastery emptied by Henry VIII after he had executed one of the monks in a public and sickening way at Tyburn, hung, drawn and quartered for a religious disagreement, gutted while still alive, a terrible punishment. But the monk had revenge.

When Henry died in 1547 his coffin was placed in the monastic church at Syon to rest overnight on its way to interment at Windsor and two guards reported hearing an explosion from inside the coffin. When they went to investigate they found that the coffin's lead seal had burst open when the gases in the decomposing body exploded and a dog was licking the dead sovereign's blood, and other things, from the floor.

The strange thing was that this appalling event fulfilled a prophecy that Henry would pay for the terrible things he had done by having his body eaten by dogs after he died. The following morning the plumbers were sent for and the coffin was sealed again before being taken on the rest of its journey to Windsor. It's a horrifying tale and I'm going to have nightmares tonight!

"Now then Amy," says Robert, "I know what you're thinking but the monastery's no longer there. Somerset demolished it when he built his new house on the same site. So come now, let's not be foolish."

"Well the house didn't bring poor Somerset much luck either. But I don't suppose your father cared about that. He was the one who profited."

There's a moment's pause before Robert's indignant outburst. "And so have you profited, my fine lady. I didn't hear your objections to wealth at our expensive wedding at Sheen Palace, which, I would like to remind you, is not a dagger's throw from Syon where you now refuse to go! Now you put on airs and graces and pretend false fancies. Oh, how you've changed Amy! Go back to your own father's tumbledown manor house at Syderstone if you're too precious to do **my** father's bidding in a time of need."

"You know very well that we never lived at Syderstone. I lived with my mother at Stanfield Hall, Robert. Have you forgotten?" snaps Amy, "And you were only too eager to visit me there, as I recall."

"Stanfield or Syderstone. Go back to the fields of Norfolk if you don't wish to give me the support a husband deserves. Otherwise you **will** obey me!" Robert is shouting ever more loudly.

There's a silence and the sound of weeping.

"I'm sorry, Robert. Forgive me. You're quite right. I do want to be a good wife to you and I will join you and do your father's bidding. It's just that ..... we are so seldom together these days. You are at court all the time and I stay here with Kate for company. At least here I'm closer to you and I do see you sometimes - but if we move to Syon, I'm so afraid that I'll be left there when you return to court; you here in London and me nine miles up the road at Richmond. That's not how a husband and wife should live, always apart. No wonder we have no children, Robin." Amy uses the affectionate form of address that she always uses when she's trying to manipulate Robert.

"My sweet Amy, why would I want to be away from you? Listen, Amy. There's a reason my father is calling the family together. Things are happening quickly and we have to act. The young King Edward is dying and will not last the week and you may yet have a brother-in-law as King of all England. How would that suit you? My family will no longer be the servants of kings, we will be kings ourselves! But, Amy, you must not breathe a word of this to anyone, not even to your good friend, Kate. My dear wife, don't you understand? Elizabeth and Mary will be nothing. You need not give a fig for Elizabeth. My brother, Guildford, and Lady Jane will be King and Queen before the end of July. Just mark my words."

When I hear this, my blood runs cold. This has to be Northumberland's most ambitious scheme yet to further the Dudley family, and the most dangerous. Robert and his loveable younger brother, Guildford, are right at the heart of the conspiracy and their wives, Amy and the highly intellectual Lady Jane, will be implicated with them in the plot. It strikes terror into my heart. The punishment for women involved in treason and plotting is burning, the most dreadful death anyone could imagine. What will

26

become of us all? Where will Northumberland's ambition end?

After some whispering, there's silence then giggling next door. Amy and Robert always make up their quarrels in bed, so Amy tells me. But I cannot sleep. Robert's father is playing a dangerous game. Doesn't he realise that the people will want Edward's half sister, the Lady Mary, as Queen? The Duke of Northumberland must be completely out of touch with the popular mood in London. His plotting will bring us all down with him.

Chapter Two
A Change of Plan

That night sleep evades me. I lie tossing and turning, sometimes dozing a little, descending into nightmares where Amy, Jane and I are surrounded by flames and we're trying to run away from a man dressed in black. We're screaming and begging for pardon as the flames lick round our feet. I wake again in a sweat and then I'm half dreaming that we are back at Stanfield in the peaceful countryside of Norfolk, far away from the machinations at court.

I awake once more with a start and look at the window. It's July and the nights are short. Soon I see the first grey light of dawn and hear the birds singing outside.

There's a knock on my door and Amy saunters in. She's looking very pleased with herself as she jumps on my bed, spreads her nightgown over her knees and sits smiling at my bleary eyes.

"I've got something to tell you," she says in teasing voice.

I can hardly say, "I know," without her realising that I've heard all the conversation from the previous night, although how she can think that anyone could **not** have heard, I can't imagine.

"We're going to Syon House immediately," she says, "Robert is with the grooms, organising things. The horses are being saddled as we speak."

"I thought you didn't like Syon."

"I don't but it's very important. All the Dudleys will be there and the Council too. Can you keep a little secret?"

Inwardly I sigh. Poor Robert! Did he for one moment think that Amy could keep news of such momentous importance to herself? I let her explain and, when she's finished, I say, "But how can Robert's father think to depose King Edward when the poor young man's not yet dead? This is treason and we'll all suffer for it."

"Ah, but he *soon will be dead*, Kate," says Amy.

"No! You're quite wrong. The King was seen at the window of Greenwich Palace a few days ago. The news was that he's still very ill but not close to death. He may yet recover."

"My dear Katherine, sweet Kat, how simple you are! Robert told me everything as we lay in bed last night. His last appearance was a plot to make him appear healthier than he was. The news of his true state of health has been suppressed so that the succession will go smoothly with no interference from Mary."

"But the Council will decide upon the Princess Mary. King Henry left provision for the succession before he died and made it a law passed by parliament; first Edward, his son by Jane Seymour, then his two daughters, Mary and Elizabeth. The people love Mary as they loved her mother, Queen Katherine of Aragon. They'll want no other Queen."

"The people will have whoever the Council says they will have and Robert says that King Edward wishes it to be Lady Jane. She's Edward's cousin and perfectly acceptable and both Mary and Elizabeth are the bastard daughters of divorced mothers." Amy says this with a certain amount of relish and a satisfied smile.

"Besides," she says, "Jane's an evangelical and follows the new religion, as does Edward and all of us. The people will not want a return to the old religion and Mary is a devout Catholic."

This isn't quite what I've heard among the servants. They tell me that many people in London would welcome a return to the old religion just as long as the monarch was head of the church and not the Pope in Rome. And they have a lot of sympathy for Mary. I think, but I don't say, that maybe the Dudleys are out of touch with the popular mood in the country.

"Has the Duke told Princess Mary of her brother's imminent death?" I ask.

"No," says Amy excitedly, "That's the best bit. She still thinks her brother is ill but not close to death and Robert's father has asked her to come to London to visit him at his sickbed."

"Why would he do that?"

"So he can arrest Mary and imprison her in the Tower of course. She won't be able to cause much mischief there!"

There's someone at the door and Amy makes shushing sounds but it's only her maid, Mrs Picto, who is carrying her dress for the day, a riding outfit with a green velvet gown and a hat to match. Amy's very fond of beautiful clothes and likes to look her best on all occasions. As Mrs Picto helps us on with our fine stockings, shifts, kirtles and bodices, another young servant comes into the chamber and curtseys to Amy, presenting her with a posy of flowers and lavender from "dear Robin" as Amy calls him delightedly. Among the flowers are two twigs from an oak tree. It's a joke. The Latin words for oak are quercus robur; 'oak Robert', laughs his wife.

It's not yet six in the morning but we're to leave immediately. We'll be at Syon in just two hours time and will not eat until we arrive there. Riding on a full stomach is most unpleasant.

In the courtyard downstairs the grooms have the horses ready and liveried men wait to accompany us. Robert lifts Amy into the saddle of the horse he gave her just before they were married, a little grey mare he'd schooled himself. He's a fine horseman and, like all the men in his family, tall, athletic and handsome. For Amy he was quite a catch!

A groom lifts me onto my horse and Robert mounts Valiant, the high stepping black Spanish stallion that is his pride and joy. No one can ride him but his master and even the grooms give his prancing feet a wide berth. Half a dozen of Robert's men are to accompany us on our journey. The streets are quiet at this time of day but outside London brigands lurk in the woods and along the roadside. With a clatter of hooves in the courtyard we're off.

At the house of Amy's mother, Stanfield Hall, we led a pleasant but not over-indulgent life. She'd married Amy's father when her first husband died and left her with young children. Stanfield was hers and Amy's father, a wealthy gentleman farmer called Sir John Robsart, left his own manor house, Syderstone, which was in a considerable state of disrepair, to live at Stanfield.

I joined the Robsarts when my mother, a distant relative of Sir John, died and my father left for Calais. I never saw him again. Amy and her half brothers and sisters were my kin as I grew up and, because

Amy and I were the same age, I went with her when she married Lord Robert to be her gentlewoman companion.

At Stanfield we'd learned to ride the two white mules owned by Amy's mother, Lady Elizabeth. Sir John rode one of the heavy horses, so popular in Norfolk, around his farm lands. And there were also two ponies, Meg and Molly, which had been childhood favourites with all of us. But neither Amy nor I could ride well until she met Robert Dudley. He trained two quiet horses for us to ride and gave us riding lessons. Now we canter along and go over small ditches and streams laughing and screaming (which Robert tells us we should not do if we are to become proper horsewomen!) but I doubt that we will ever hunt and ride the way the royal ladies, Mary and Elizabeth, do.

As we ride out of the courtyard and over the cobble stones we're silent, lost in thought, but we've barely gone three hundred yards when there's the sound of another person riding hard along the dirt road behind us. His horse skids to an abrupt halt in a cloud of dust and Amy irritably brushes the dirt from her gown. It's Robert's brother, Ambrose.

"Robert, things are happening. Father needs you at Durham Place – straight away," says Ambrose after the usual courtesies to Amy and me.

"Oh well I suppose it's better than Syon," remarks Amy, turning her horse's head back to Somerset House.

"I beg your pardon, Amy," says Ambrose, "But the Duke wants no one but Robert. Some of the Privy Counsellors are there and this is not a meeting in which women can play any part."

Rebuffed and annoyed, Amy rides her horse back along the road to Somerset House, passing the gate to Durham Place on the way. She enters the courtyard without a farewell to either Robert or his brother and I follow her. I can see she's seething. The men follow us while Robert accompanies Ambrose through the gates of Durham Place.

One of the grooms helps Amy down from her horse and she tosses her reins over to him and goes striding back into the house removing her gloves. I hasten to catch up. When we get inside she flings her gloves down on the table and marches upstairs and down the Long Gallery to a small chamber overlooking the gardens. I close the door behind me.

"He's always doing this, always," she rants, once we are safely inside and the door is closed.

"Who is?"

"The Duke. Who else? He thinks he can do as he pleases."

"Well, he can, can't he? And he must have a reason for wanting Robert so urgently."

"He uses him like an animal. He may as well put a bridle on him."

I let her go on in this way. I guess that, having said she didn't want to go to Syon, she'd been curious to find out what was happening there and was looking forward to a ride out with her husband anyway; a rare pleasure, now missed, and her second disappointment in two days. There's a knock on the door. Amy looks up eagerly. Has Robert returned for her?

Two servants come in with plates of cold meat, bread, honey cakes and warm spiced wine. It should cheer her up but it doesn't. Amy looks around for the sugar to put into her wine. It's a disgusting habit she picked up at court.

"At least we don't have to have breakfast at Durham Place," I say. "I hope the cook doesn't poison half the Council at the meeting."

Amy nearly chokes on her wine with laughter at this. Her foul mood is temporarily broken.

"He may just serve them salad again!"

We dissolve into fits of giggling at our private joke. A few weeks earlier Robert's brother, Guilford, had married Lady Jane Grey at Durham Place. In fact it had been a triple wedding celebration with Robert's youngest sister, Katherine, and Jane's sister, also named Katherine, marrying at the same time. Durham Place with its beautiful marble pillars was an opulent setting for the weddings – no wonder Northumberland was so eager to take the palace from Elizabeth! What's more the banquets were quite unbelievable with food of every kind, venison pies, roast beef, mutton, capons, pigeon and pheasant, larks and swans garnished with spices and salad leaves, almond tarts, jellies, junket and custards, marzipan in the shape of tiny fruits. There were pageants and masques with dancing in the evening. A wonderful celebration indeed! Except for one thing!

A good number of the guests were very ill afterwards and the shame faced Duke accused the cook of mistaking one salad leaf for another leaf which was poisonous. Amy and I were not at all ill; we hate salad!

"William Cecil's face was green!" laughs Amy.

"It's a good thing the King was too ill to attend. Can you imagine if your father in law had finished him off? Everyone would have said it was a deliberate attempt to replace the monarch by poisoning him."

This sobers us up considerably. It might just have happened too and the consequences would have been too dreadful to contemplate even though the Duke would never think of harming King Edward. Some of the guests were still very ill two weeks later and many said that it was a bad omen for Guildford and Jane.

Amy and I eat our breakfast deep in thought. Then we while away the morning talking about Jane Grey. She's a strange one and we find it hard to make her out. First of all she's so serious; it's said that she's the most highly educated woman in the country and she's just sixteen! Not much fun to be with though!

"You can say what you like but I think you can have too much studying," says Amy, who's sensitive to the fact that, while she was well educated by Norfolk standards, she's quite a dullard compared to ladies such as Jane and Elizabeth.

Jane shared some of her lessons with the King himself; they are almost the same age and second cousins. Elizabeth and Robert had also been educated at court and by the same tutors. They were both bright and gifted scholars who were friends from the age of eight; Amy knows this and resents it. She feels left out and Elizabeth, it seems, on the few occasions that she and Amy have met, takes great pleasure in talking to Robert in Latin in Amy's presence. Amy's provincial tutoring means that her Latin is not up to their level. What's more she has a strong Norfolk accent, a subject of much amusement among some of Robert's friends. And Elizabeth knows this and

35

delights in the fact that Robert's wife is made to feel inferior.

"Jane says that her parents insisted that she had to be the best at everything, even when she was dancing," I say.

"I feel sorry for her," says Amy, "She says if she showed any pleasure she was criticised for enjoying herself too much and not trying hard enough. She says they used to pinch her if she did anything wrong."

"Her parents have high hopes of her. She's the eldest girl and they have no boys. At least they've given her an education fit for ...."

"A Queen?"

"I was going to say 'fit for a boy'."

"They say the King wants her to be Queen after him and he's written it in his will, his own device for the succession," says Amy.

"Hm! I wonder if that was Edward's own idea. It sounds like Northumberland to me. Is that why the Duke wanted her married to Guildford - so that his own son could be king?"

"That's what they're saying at court – not in front of Northumberland of course. They say that the Duke persuaded Edward to choose Jane as his heir to make Guildford king. King Guildford! It doesn't sound right, does it?"

"Not to me. Where are Guildford and Jane now?"

"Until a few days ago they were living in Katherine Parr's old house in Chelsea."

"And they're still there?"

"Who knows? With Northumberland anything can happen."

We then travel down another path in our conversation and start to discuss the mentor of Jane Grey, Katherine Parr, and her strange life, her marriage to Henry VIII and how close she came to execution for her strong evangelical views and for disagreeing strongly with Henry over this. We talk about her friend, Anne Askew, who was tortured in the Tower in a failed attempt to make her implicate Katherine in holding treasonous views (that is to say, views contrary to Henry's views) on religious reform.

And then we recall in fascinated horror the story of how Anne's broken body was finally tied to a chair and fastened to the stake where she was burned for her refusal to inform on Katherine Parr and the rest of her friends.

Of course we cannot remember all this. We were small children at the time. But the people remembered and the story of Anne Askew passed into the realm of folk lore. Never before or since has a woman been tortured on the rack. It brought shame to Henry in the eyes of the people.

But it terrified Katherine Parr who apologised to her husband for her wayward views and was ultimately saved by Henry's very timely death. She then shocked everyone by marrying her old love, Thomas Seymour – the same Thomas Seymour, later to be Earl of Sudeley, who had indulged in scandalously inappropriate behaviour with the young Elizabeth while Katherine was pregnant with his child.

Elizabeth left the house in disgrace but another person, loyal to Katherine Parr, stayed and this was their other ward, a very young girl - named Jane, the same Lady Jane Grey who is now Amy's sister-in-law. It's a small world!

Jane had been Katherine Parr's most trusted companion, even though she was just twelve at the time, and had taken in Katherine's very advanced views on religious reform. Fortunately the new King Edward shared their views so they no longer had any need to fear the bonfire or the executioner's axe. Edward's introduction of a new English Prayer Book had fulfilled all Katherine's dreams.

But, after the Elizabeth scandal, tragedy struck. Jane had travelled with the pregnant Katherine to Sudeley House in Gloucestershire and remained with her during her confinement. Jane had loved the huge library there and the birth of the child was eagerly anticipated. But her role was not to be that of older 'sister' to the baby; instead she became chief mourner at Katherine's funeral when the poor woman died of fever soon after giving birth.

Jane had been in her twelfth year at the time of the funeral but she had learned many valuable lessons from the time spent in the care of the generous and kindly Katherine. She became her own person, strong in her views to the point of rudeness to those who disagreed with them. She grew into a mature woman and was old beyond her years by the time she married the much loved and doted upon Guildford, younger brother of Robert Dudley.

Oh yes, Amy and I agree, Jane has seen life in all its perverse vagaries and is no fool; she will not allow Northumberland to dominate her. She had been fortunate to have a very good teacher in Katherine Parr whose circle of intelligent and free thinking women friends had refused to be dominated by their husbands, even if poor Anne Askew had paid a terrible price for her courageous belief in the rights of women to hold an educated opinion.

"If a woman can't hold a view without fear of her husband calling her a heretic," I say, "I think I'd rather not be married. Just imagine! You're voicing your thoughts based on your studies of the new learning and the next thing your husband, whose probably got his eye on someone younger anyway, is turning you in to the religious authorities as a heretic so you can be burned and got rid of. Much to his convenience, of course! Very nice for him!"

"Robert would never do that to me, Kate," says Amy.

"That's because you got married for love, Amy, and not because your parents told you to. Do you remember Cecil's pompous comment at your wedding? 'I don't believe in carnal marriages' he said. It's his favourite saying!"

"Yes. He should talk! His first marriage was exactly that and his own parents didn't even approve."

"Well anyway his first wife was lucky enough to die. Just imagine having to live with him, the old sour face," I smile grimly. We both laugh.

"But seriously," Amy says, "Jane doesn't seem to be averse to Guildford, even though it was an arranged wedding. But I know for a fact that she can't stand her new father-in-law, Northumberland."

"There will be interesting times ahead," asserts Amy as we walk around the gardens in the mid morning sunshine.

She never spoke a truer word.

Chapter Three
The Dudleys Close Rank

Just before midday Amy and I go into the house to eat dinner. We do not dine with the servants in the Great Hall, as is the custom when the master or mistress of the house is present. Instead we take our dinner in the withdrawing room upstairs. The cook has prepared a stew of young rabbit and with the fine manchet bread, it's delicious. There are little tarts of preserved quince jelly to follow the meat.

"You should not add sugar to your wine," I reprimand her.

"Why not? They do at court."

"Only because they can then drink more and be merry. The goings-on in the evenings at court are a scandal! Foreign visitors are disgusted."

Amy shrugs. "I don't drink too much anyway," she says. It's true and I feel mean for spoiling her pleasure. Robert is often away on court business and, apart from me, she's on her own and lonely.

After our dinner we settle down to a game of cards but very soon we hear the sound of hooves outside. Amy leaps up.

"Robert," she says excitedly.

But it isn't; it's his brother, Ambrose, and he's alone. We watch from the window as he dismounts and strides towards the main entrance. Amy goes running down the Long Gallery to meet him.

"Ambrose. What's the news? What's happening?"

Ambrose puts a finger to his lips and looks over his shoulder to ensure we're alone. We go back into the withdrawing room and Amy pours three glasses from the flagon ….. and adds sugar to her glass.

"That's a distasteful habit," says Ambrose. Amy pulls a face and shrugs.

"Well," he says, "Let's start at the beginning. Robert asked me to beg your forgiveness, Amy, for he can not return home this evening."

Amy's face reveals her disappointment ….. and anger. But she keeps quiet, awaiting Ambrose's explanation.

"King Edward is within hours of death."

"God rest his soul," says Amy and I say, "Amen" to that.

"He will not live to see another day. Our sister Mary and her husband, Henry Sidney, are with him as we speak. Henry holds the poor boy in his arms and tries to comfort him. Edward is in terrible pain; he coughs up black, foul-smelling matter and is covered in sores. His death will be a merciful release."

We are all three silent as we reflect on the sad, short life of the poor young man. Jane Seymour, his mother, had died soon after he was born. His father, King Henry, had died when he was ten and then Edward had been prevented by his uncle, Edward Seymour, Duke of Somerset, from seeing his step mother, Katherine Parr, Henry's sixth wife, who had been motherly and warm towards him. Then his cousin, Jane Grey, with whom he had grown up at court and of whom he had become very fond, was made a ward of his other uncle, Thomas Seymour, Earl of Sudeley, and his new wife – none other than Katherine, Henry's widow. So Edward lost Jane's company too.

Everyone the young King had loved had been taken away from him by the scheming adults at his court. Finally his uncle Thomas Sudeley was executed for treason, followed not long afterwards by his uncle Edward, Duke of Somerset. Now the only one of his former friends left at court is Henry Sidney, his comforter as he lies dying. It's cause for reflection. Who would be a king?

"Poor boy!" I say and Ambrose nods but then he says,

"What I am to tell you now is a matter for our kin and for no other ears. As far as I am concerned you are our kin too, Kate." He gives both Amy and me a serious, direct look.

"Edward has made Lady Jane Grey his heir. Not her male descendants, as he originally wanted, but Lady Jane herself. He has stated specifically that he does not want either Mary or Elizabeth, as Mary will restore Catholicism and the ties to the Pope in Rome and Elizabeth was the whore Anne Boleyn's daughter. Both of them, he says, may marry a foreign prince and England may lose its sovereignty if either one is Queen."

"Robert told me of Edward's 'device' for the succession," says Amy, "So where does the problem lie? It's what the King wanted."

"The problem," says Ambrose, "Is that some members of the Privy Council say that Edward's device was not ratified by Parliament and is therefore illegal. The only legal document was King Henry's Succession which stated that first Mary and then Elizabeth were to be his heirs should Edward die childless. They say it would be an act of treason to declare Jane to be Queen."

"So what will happen next?"

"We can do nothing before Edward dies, which, pray God, will be mercifully soon. He suffers so. Father believes it will be a simple matter to win over the dissenters on the Privy Council. He has many allies for Jane already. But first he has plans to arrest the Lady Mary and prevent her from causing trouble. He informed her that Edward is very ill and wishes to see her. He had hoped to detain her when she came to court. Unfortunately Mary seems to have smelled the plot and remains at her home, twenty miles away, at Hunsdon."

"And Robert? Where does he fit into your father's plotting?"

"Please show more respect towards the Duke, your father-in-law," Ambrose speaks severely to Amy. "Robert has been dispatched to Hunsdon with a small army of horsemen to arrest the Lady Mary there."

"WHAT?" shrieks Amy, just about as disrespectfully as she can. "The Duke has sent Robert to do his dirty work for him. Why could he not go himself? Why not John? Why not you, Ambrose? You are both his older brothers. It's not fair to send Robert. If it all goes badly, it's Robert who will suffer a traitor's death. How can the Duke do this to his own son?" Amy's voice tails off into a wail of despair.

"Take heart, Amy," says Ambrose, "You know that I am fond of Robert too. We are very close and father has said that there is nothing to fear from Mary. She will either be arrested at Hunsdon or she will flee and escape to the continent and the protection of the Emperor, Charles, her kinsman. The French have promised help for our cause. They do not wish to see Mary made Queen and will do anything against the Hapsburg Empire. They fear Mary's Spanish blood will give the Emperor a foothold in England."

Amy looks doubtful and a tear rolls down her cheek. What Ambrose says is reassuring and yet …… Can the French be trusted? But it makes sense that Mary would flee to her cousin, the Holy Roman Emperor, the Hapsburg Charles V, who now rules most of Europe. The French hate him and the Hapsburg dynasty even more than they mistrust the English.

"Don't worry," says Ambrose, "Father has the matter completely in hand. Nothing could be more certain. Tomorrow he will persuade the remaining Council members to support him – they will not dare refuse – and the rest will go smoothly." He pauses. "Finally I am here, Amy, to ask you as a member of our kin to support us by offering your assistance."

"What does the Duke wish me to do?" Amy says this with an air of resignation.

"As soon as the King dies, Lady Jane Grey is to be taken to Syon House by my sister, Mary Sidney. They will travel up the Thames by wherry from Katherine Parr's old house at Chelsea. Father intended us all to be at Syon to welcome Jane but with the recent turn of events, Mary Tudor's reluctance to come to court and the Council's wavering in its support, the Duke and my brothers are all needed here in London. The King's death will not be announced until everyone is united and all is complete."

"Everyone is needed at court except Robert whose life, it seems, is expendable. He does the dirty business of arresting the person some would see as the rightful Queen," says Amy bitterly.

Ambrose ignores this latest jibe. "It is certain the King will die in the next few hours so Jane and Mary will go to Syon tomorrow. Father wishes Jane to have some people there of her own age. He would like you and Kate to join Jane and Mary in the evening. It will make Jane feel more comfortable and you may take a wherry up river from Somerset House."

With that Ambrose gets up and takes his leave of us. We've not been asked to help by his father, Northumberland, we have been ordered. Amy is not the least bit reassured by the news of Robert and I feel very apprehensive for the two of us. One way or another we are involved in the Dudleys' plotting up to our ears.

Chapter Four
Syon

The following morning we pack a few possessions into a small wooden box. We don't expect to stay at Syon for long and we sleep in the shifts we wear under our kirtles and gowns so we need very little other than a comb and our small pieces of jewellery. Then we begin another seemingly interminable wait for Ambrose's servant to arrive. It's well into the afternoon before he escorts us down to the wharf where the wherries are waiting.

The journey upstream takes time. It's a pleasant journey and the weather is fair. A kingfisher skims the water and, as we leave the city behind, there are few boats other than ours. No one speaks. Conversation in front of the servants may give too much away.

Finally we round a bend in the river and there in front of us is Sheen which means 'beautiful place'. It's the royal palace where Amy and Robert were married three years ago. King Edward had attended the wedding and so had his sister Elizabeth on what was an extravagant occasion of feasting and entertainment and it makes me sad as I remember how the young king had been almost childish in his delight at the masques, pageants and jousting. Presumably he has now died or we would not be making this journey.

I glance at Amy's face as she too gazes at the magnificent façade of the palace. I wonder what she's thinking. Her marriage has taken her to the very heart of the court and she now has wealth and position that most women would envy but she has little personal happiness. She loves her husband very much and, indeed, I think that he loves her too but ….. he is always working. They see so little of each other and I know that they would dearly like a child.

Sheen is a little way up river and situated on the southern bank; we swing away from it as the oarsmen pull towards the northern bank where there is a landing stage for Syon House. They hold the wherry steady as we disembark.

Like Somerset House, Syon is imposing and new; although the ruins of the abbey can be clearly seen alongside it.

"It makes me shudder," says Amy breaking the silence.

We walk from the landing stage up the path to the imposing entrance where Jane Grey (now Jane Dudley) and Mary Sidney, Amy's sister in law, are waiting to greet us on the steps.

"You knew we were coming?" says Amy.

"No, we saw you walking up the path," says Mary. "Jane has been so anxious; we were in the Long Gallery watching from all the windows for any sign of someone approaching."

Amy then remembers the servants and dismisses them. We wait until they've gone round to the kitchen entrance before continuing.

"When we arrived here there was no one to greet us," says Jane. "We are the only occupants of the house apart from the servants. I thought we had been lured into a trap, empty house and everything. I feared that Mary Tudor had sent us here. I …. I thought she planned to murder me."

So does Jane have any idea of the real reason she's here, I'm wondering. Surely she must suspect something, and yet ….

"Do you have any news of the King," asks Amy.

"Edward died last night. He complained about feeling faint and just died in Henry's arms as they said a prayer together," says Mary.

"God rest his soul," Amy and I murmur in unison.

"Amen," says Jane.

So Jane does know of the King's death.

"And now?" says Amy.

"We wait for the Duke," says Mary simply.

We go into the palace and enter a chamber where the servants have laid out platters of cold meats and bread. Amy's face brightens considerably.

"I think we should all go to the chapel before supper," says Jane, "And offer some prayers for God's guidance in this. We need not pray for Edward. He died in faith and will receive his reward in heaven." Amy's face is a picture but she can hardly refuse. Jane is soon to be her Queen!

We walk along to the little chapel. The walls are bare and free of pictures and the altar is a simple wooden table by the wall. There are no candles or silverware in the new evangelical style of worship. Jane has the new prayer book, written in English on Edward's instructions. She leads the prayers and we pray on our knees for a long time, Amy shuffling uncomfortably. I wonder if her thoughts are straying back to the supper table!

Finally Jane says Archbishop Cranmer's beautiful evening prayer, "Lighten our darkness, we beseech thee, O Lord, and, by Thy great mercy, defend us from all perils and danger of this night. For the love

of thy only Son, our Saviour, Jesus Christ our Lord."
For a while we remain frozen in time, motionless and
silent as we reflect on the meaning. It's a prayer that
we all appreciate for we are in great peril at this
uncertain time.

When we get back to the chamber where our
supper was laid out, it's disappeared! Amy is very
annoyed but Jane remarks that she wasn't hungry
anyway so we have to go along with that. And it's no
use complaining to the servants. They will have
assumed, as is the custom, that we have finished with
the dishes and that what remains is theirs. Our supper
will have been consumed some time ago but not by
us!

No one feels like playing cards and we have no
needle work to keep us employed. We walk up and
down the Long Gallery a few times talking quietly
and then retire to bed. Mary is sleeping in the
chamber next to Jane and Amy and I are sharing a
bed in the next chamber. A woman servant is
summoned to help Jane with her clothes and then she
offers her services to us but we don't need her. Amy
and I can help each other.

Syon, like Somerset House, is clean and new and
barely used. The garderobes or privies smell sweet
even though it is now mid summer and Amy quickly
checks our bed for bed bugs, whisking back the
covers. Normally we see several of them running
underneath the mattress ready to plague us with bites
later in the night while we are sleeping; but here all is
new and there are no fleas or bugs. We heave a sigh
of relief; we will have a good night's sleep. We
climb into bed in our shifts, our only items of
underwear.

Somehow I doubt that Jane will sleep soundly tonight.

The next day we arise early. Amy is ravenously hungry and determined not to miss her breakfast which, fortunately, is substantial. Almost immediately things start to happen as people arrive at Syon. First is the Duke of Northumberland himself. I have to say that he is very affectionate towards his children and that the Dudleys are all close and loving towards each other. He gives his married daughter, Mary Sidney, a warm embrace and kisses her fondly on the cheek. Amy and I get a salutary bow and we curtsey in return.

Other members of the Privy Council arrive, Pembroke, Northampton, Arundel and Huntingdon. When all are assembled Northumberland, who has been talking to his daughter all this time, ushers Jane into a chamber and the Council members follow. Now Amy seizes her opportunity to find out the latest news.

"What did the Duke say, Mary?"

"The good news is that the Mayor of London and the city magistrates agreed to support Jane only yesterday morning at Greenwich, where the body of the King now lies. They have sworn an oath of allegiance to her. Most members of the Council also said they will acknowledge Jane's right to the throne and the ones that disagree say they will not cause trouble."

"So all is well then?"

"Not quite," says Mary. "The imperial ambassador, Renard, and others have leaked the news of the King's death and now word is spreading around London before we are ready to make an

50

announcement. And Robert arrived at Hunsdon to discover that the Lady Mary Tudor had escaped to Cambridge on the pretence that she was fleeing a plague of sickness at Hunsdon. Now Robert and his men will have to follow her across the countryside if they wish to apprehend her."

From the chamber where Northumberland and the other Councillors are talking to Jane there is the sound of voices in discussion. The Duke emerges and asks for Jane's mother to be brought. She soon arrives with the Duchess of Northumberland and Northampton's wife who enter the chamber with the others. Eventually they all emerge smiling, except for Jane who's as serious as ever. She does not acknowledge her friends of the previous evening as we curtsey. Every man present kneels before her.

The following day Mary Sidney tells us that Northumberland is to address a large gathering of members of the Privy Council, nobles and their wives here at Syon. The Duke will formally state Edward's wishes for the succession and will offer Jane the crown in front of all the assembled gathering. And Jane, of course, will accept.

Unfortunately Amy and I will not be present on this momentous occasion. As Jane and her followers make their way to the Great Hall for supper, Mary Sidney prevents us from joining them.

"I'm sorry, Amy and Kate," she says, "Father has asked me to tell you that your loyalty will not be forgotten and that you are to go back to Somerset House immediately where you will receive further instructions tomorrow or on Monday."

Amy does not need to collect her jewellery from her little box upstairs; not to be overshadowed, she's wearing the lot! She turns abruptly on her heel and I follow her.

Chapter Five
The Tower

Even by Amy's standards I don't think I've ever seen her so annoyed. She's always felt that Robert's parents regard her as far beneath them and this confirms it. She's been excluded from all the ceremony and celebration at Syon.

"Had Robert been here," she complains bitterly, "They would have been obliged to include both of us. They wish me to know I am nothing without him. Had he married the daughter of a nobleman it would have been different."

To make matters worse no one seems to know where Robert is or what he's doing. Amy's only consolation seems to be that Elizabeth has remained at her house at Hatfield apparently and is just as excluded as we are.

When we walk through the door at Somerset House there's a buzz of excitement among the servants.

"Oh Mistress Katherine," says Bess, the house keeper, "Do you know the news? The poor King has died and Lady Mary will now be Queen. There's talk of nothing else in the city."

Yes, well! What am I to say to that?

"Except that," says Joan, the house maid, "Some people," she lowers her voice, "Say that the Duke of Northumberland has a plot to make his own son, Lord Guildford, king!"

Oh no! It's as bad as that!

"Don't be silly, Joan," I say, "That's foolish talk. How can the Duke make Guildford king when he has no line of succession to the throne?"

Amy orders supper for us. It's very late and we're worn out with considering all the complexities and uncertainties of Northumberland's plot. After supper we retire to bed.

The following morning is Sunday so we go to Paul's Cross to hear the Bishop of London, Nicholas Ridley, preach. It's an attempt on our behalf to ascertain the mood in the city. Far away from Syon where Northumberland has made a speech to a submissive group of councillors and nobles declaring Edward's wishes for the succession and the right of Jane's claim to the throne, Ridley shockingly preaches, to a very different crowd, that Mary and Elizabeth are bastards. The congregation is not impressed by his language. His support of Jane falls on deaf ears and there are mutterings and murmurings among the people.

"Northumberland's dog," says one man.

"His downfall is coming," says another.

Amy and I slip away before we are questioned. Despite the guards standing around to protect Ridley we feel very vulnerable. Even the evangelicals seem to opt for Mary so where will our support come from? We have a very bad feeling.

Mary Sidney comes to Somerset House that evening. She tells us what has happened at Syon but we do not say what we've been hearing in the city. Apparently, says Mary, it came as a shock to Jane to be offered the crown of England for she fell down in a fit of crying.

"That doesn't sound like Jane!" says Amy cynically. "She may be only sixteen but she's tougher than that."

Privately I agree. There's a tale that Jane once entered the house of the Lady Mary Tudor with her mother, the Duchess of Suffolk, and insulted, to Mary's face and in her own home, Mary's manner of worship with candles and ornaments on the altar. Despite the fact she was still a young girl, she was blunt to the point of rudeness and her mother was left to apologise. No; Jane is not the fragile weeping sort. More likely she made a calculated, dramatic and public gesture to express her own reluctance to take the crown. That way she would have plenty of witnesses that she had not wished for it should everything go wrong later! Hm! Crafty Jane!

Mary tells us that everyone knelt before Jane and then there'd been a huge banquet where the new Queen sat underneath the panoply of state, a huge cloth made of rich silks and supported on poles. Amy's face darkens as she remembers the insult of being sent home the previous evening and thus missing all this. Mary, noticing, says, "Amy, the Duke my father had such limited accommodation at Syon it wasn't possible for all of us to stay. However he wishes you to attend a dinner at Durham Place at midday tomorrow when Jane will dine with us dressed in the royal robes now being laid out for her at Westminster Palace. After the dinner we will all follow her to the Tower to await her coronation."

Amy brightens considerably at this. "What about Kate?" she asks.

"Katherine can come too. The Duke wants a great show of unity for Jane."

When Mary's gone Amy rushes to choose a suitable gown. She has plenty to choose from. I have her old ones but, with Amy's love of clothes, this is no hardship. We are both very fortunate and wear all our wealth conspicuously, showing off our rich clothing and our jewellery.

The following day is Monday, 10th July. Jane, or Queen Jane as we must now call her, is brought down the Thames from Syon to Westminster Palace where she changes into her royal robes. We dress in our finest gowns and make our way to nearby Durham Place where we prepare to greet her. The Duke seems particularly agitated over something but he recovers his composure when Queen Jane arrives.

All the Dudleys are there with the exception of Robert who is still pursuing Mary in Norfolk. The banquet is sumptuous and Durham Place is a magnificent setting for the young Queen to start the path to her reign. After we have dined, the Privy Council meets to discuss urgent matters and then we make our way in procession to the wharf where the royal barge is waiting to take Jane to the Tower where she will await her coronation. Amy and I, together with other ladies of the court, take one of the boats that will form a flotilla of tiny wherries and covered barges, all accompanying Jane. There are many onlookers but they are all ominously silent. The people have guessed what's happening and there's no cheering.

At the wharf by the Tower, Northumberland, with other members of the Privy Council, is already waiting on the steps to greet the Queen. It takes a long time for the boats to land their privileged cargo and it takes even longer for the procession to form. Two hours after setting off from Durham Place we stand at the huge entrance gates to the Tower of London. Crowds are watching the display of nobility and courtiers in silence and, of course, there has, as yet, been no official announcement.

I cannot help reflecting that Jane cuts a fairly insignificant figure despite her royal robes and ermine. Had it been Elizabeth or Mary they would surely have paraded in front of the crowd on magnificent prancing horses, demonstrating their strength and horsemanship, proving themselves equal to any man.

Jane, on the other hand, has never been interested in riding and hunting, quite unlike her parents, the Duke and Duchess of Suffolk, who both love the outdoor life. It is said that Jane tried to make up for their disappointment in her by devoting herself to her studies. Now this deficit in her education makes her seem a poor substitute for her two spirited and fearless female cousins.

We enter the Tower. It's a dismal old fortress and, as the gates close behind us, the mid-summer stench of the river, heavily polluted with sewage, hits us. Amy lifts the pomander that hangs from her waist and holds it close to her nose. Wherever the court travels the smell of pollution follows as a large number of people are concentrated in a small area. Simply feeding so many presents its own problems; the deadly sweating sickness and stomach illnesses are rife.

"I hope Jane's coronation takes place soon!" says Amy.

The Duke has fortified the Tower with extra munitions and guards and we're locked in for now but it's quite apparent that there will not be accommodation for everyone. Meanwhile outside the gates a proclamation is being read by heralds declaring that Jane is Queen. The crowd is strangely quiet. The heralds move on to read the proclamation elsewhere.

Later a messenger arrives with the news that Mary has fled to Kenninghall in Norfolk where she has declared herself Queen and is rallying local people and even local gentry to her cause. No wonder Northumberland was agitated at dinner. Amy gives me a worried look and whispers, "So where is Robert?"

Even worse there's a rumour around the court that the subject of the earlier meeting of the Privy Council at Durham Place was a letter from Mary declaring her own claim to the throne by her father's Act of Succession. In the letter she hints darkly that she knows of the plot against her. It's quite obvious to me that Mary is better prepared than Northumberland had thought. He's underestimated her and she won't stand aside without a fight.

My mind goes back to the autumn of 1549 when Robert first met Amy. He'd been near Stanfield Hall with his father, who was then the Earl of Warwick and had not yet assumed the title of Duke of Northumberland. A month earlier Robert, Ambrose and their father had brutally suppressed the rebellion of Robert Kett, a simple tradesman from Norwich who had gathered a large following to his cause. People were hungry following the enclosure of common land by greedy land owners who realised that the trade in wool was highly profitable. Now their sheep were grazing on land that had been owned communally by poor people for centuries. And the poor were deprived of a livelihood and a food supply.

Robert's father had dealt with the rebels harshly. And Amy's father, Sir John Robsart, had thought this was completely justified. Kett and his brother were hanged in chains in Norwich for all to see. More than three hundred rebels, who were no more than poor and starving people, were executed; many were drawn and quartered, and Norfolk ran with blood. The Dudleys were teaching the people a terrible lesson. Even the Duke of Somerset had taken pity and later passed new laws to help the poor and hungry. Norfolk's people have never forgiven Amy's father-in-law. Northumberland's brutality will be remembered down the ages.

But when the Duke and his two handsome sons arrived at Stanfield one afternoon after the rebellion, Amy met Robert and was smitten by him. All thought of the rebels disappeared as the two young Dudley boys entertained us with their horse riding skills and mock jousting. Amy gave her handkerchief to her 'champion', Robert, and laughed and clapped with delight as he bowed to her. They were soon in love with each other and Robert's father settled for this rather socially disappointing match when Amy's father, Sir John, promised to make Amy sole heir to the vast and lucrative Robsart farm lands.

Now, it seems, the people of Norfolk are punishing Robert's father for his brutality by supporting Mary and attempting to thwart the Duke's ambitions. They are rallying to Mary's cause in large numbers. And the Duke's attitude is puzzling. He is no longer agitated and now seems completely at ease with this situation and unprepared to take immediate military action. The following day he drafts many notices to the Lord Lieutenants of the counties requiring their support for Jane and ordering them to resist the claim of 'Lady Mary bastard'. Jane, sitting under the panoply of state in the royal apartments, signs these notices 'Jane the Queen'.

The second evening Amy and I leave the overcrowded and uncomfortable accommodation of the Tower and take the river boat back to Somerset House where all is serene and normal. The servants greet us with the new gossip. Notices have been put up around the city, they say, stating the terms of Edward's wishes for the succession and declaring Mary and Elizabeth illegitimate and therefore without a claim. They are shocked. And there is more scandal!

The heralds, they say, were reading the proclamation that Jane is Queen on Monday at Cheapside and a boy, named Gilbert Potter, shouted that the Princess Mary had a better claim. Gilbert was arrested and this Tuesday morning, on the orders of the Duke, his offence was read out in public, his ears nailed to the pillory and then cut off, to the horror and disgust of the crowd and the screams of the boy.

The mood in the city is turning ugly and people are blaming the Duke. Amy and I look at each other in horror. Will there be a civil war? It seems as if everyone supports Mary and we'll be on the losing side. Who will fight on Jane's side? And, adds Amy tearfully, what has happened to Robert?

Chapter Six
News from Norfolk

The next morning is Wednesday, 12th July. We don't wish to go back to the Tower but we must show support for Jane's cause. We sleep late and are awakened by the sound of drums outside the walls of Somerset House. Groups of militia are going round recruiting an army to fight for Jane. Civil war seems inevitable.

By afternoon we can postpone our visit to Jane's court no longer.

Down by the wharf a small boy is running in front of the soldiers shouting, "Fight for Queen Jane!" He's clutching something in his hand; the soldiers have given him a coin to proclaim their cause.

Outside the gates of the Tower there are women selling small bundles of lavender and sweet smelling herbs to purify the bad air. Amy and I stop to purchase these; we don't wish to get a fever. Clutching our nosegays we make our way through the crowds. It's noisy, dusty and hectic as men and weapons are brought into the Tower.

"Are we at war?" asks Amy.

"Not yet," says a courtier. "Queen Jane has decreed that anyone who does not support her is to be dealt with savagely. She's preparing her army."

So much for the pathetic little Jane, swooning and weeping when asked to accept the crown! Whoever succeeds now there will be bloodshed and executions.

"It's important to choose the right side," whispers Amy. "Find out as much as you can, Kate." We decide to separate and go in different directions.

Inside, members of the Privy Council are forming small groups and talking in hushed voices in corners and corridors where no one can hear. They look worried and all the assuredness of two days ago has disappeared. I strain my ears to catch snatches of conversation but all I get are single words, "French", "Queen of Scots", "Renard says".

Amy and I meet up again and she has had more success.

"They say that Guildford's mother and Jane's have been arguing over whether Guildford should be made king."

"Arguing! At a time like this! Are they out of their minds? What does Jane say?"

Amy looks over her shoulder. "She says that she will not have him made king. A duke maybe but not a king. And the Duchess of Northumberland is furious with her."

"I knew it," I say. "They thought Jane would be meek and mild and do what they ordered. They underestimate her. She's stronger than they think."

"Yes, but listen to this. The Lord Treasurer, Marquess of Winchester, has taken the crown jewels to Jane, completely unrequested. She was amazed as she does not wish to be crowned for another two weeks and asked him why he was doing this. He said that he thought she might wish to try them on and that she may wish a crown to be made for Guildford."

At this my mouth drops open. "Aha. I smell a rat! He's trying to cause trouble for Jane."

"Yes; but why would he do that?"

We'll have to ponder that one. It would seem that some of Jane's so called allies on the Council are not quite as loyal as we first thought.

"And there's something else," continues Amy. "There are rumours flying round that Northumberland is trying to make a secret deal with the French to ensure their support. Renard, the Imperial Ambassador, has said so."

"Your father-in-law wouldn't do that, would he?"

"He might. I wouldn't put it past him."

"Or it may just be Renard and the Hapsburgs trying to cause trouble."

"That's true."

As we return home that evening all kinds of weaponry are being taken into the Tower, large carts holding guns, spears, bows, arrows, armour, followed by men willing to fight (or willing to be paid to fight) for Jane's cause.

"Who will lead the Queen's army?" Amy asks a young lieutenant.

"The Queen's father, the Duke of Suffolk, of course," he replies.

We fight our way through crowds of sullen onlookers to get down to the wharf.

When we reach the Tower the following day the situation is very different. Queen Jane is obviously feeling the strain and the news from Norfolk is not good. The Lady Mary is at Framlingham Castle which is strongly fortified and has hundreds of men forming a huge crowd of supporters outside the walls. The gentry who have rallied to her side are organising them into an army.

The most shocking news is that Jane's father, Suffolk, who was to have led her army against Mary, is now ill and suffering from fainting fits. Jane has asked the Privy Council to choose another person and they have voted unanimously for Northumberland.

The Duke must realise that this smacks of a plot to get him out of the way but he can hardly refuse to lead the army that will support the Queen and his own son, her husband.

Guildford is to remain in the Tower with Jane while his brothers, John, Ambrose and even the sixteen year old Henry, will ride with their father and Jane's army to meet Mary's army in Norfolk. For Amy there is some good news. Having been diverted from his task of capturing Mary, Robert has been touring the towns in the north of Norfolk, around King's Lynn, to gain support for Jane and has initially gained some success. At least he's still alive.

Meanwhile at Durham Place the Duke is taking his leave of the Privy Council and reminding them of their allegiance to Queen Jane, and, by association, to himself. We learn later that each and every one of them has pledged their loyalty. He returns briefly to the Tower to take his leave of the Queen; the Earl of Arundel wishes him well and says how sorry he is that he will not be able to fight with him. There's an air of excitement now around the court as we all chatter about the events of the day and pray for a hasty conclusion to the fighting.

"It's Thursday," says Amy as we make our way home, "Do you feel like going to Southwark to watch the bear baiting?" She's obviously feeling in a lighter mood now that she knows that Robert's alive and well.

"I've had enough of crowds for one day," I say. It's true but there's another reason. While bear baiting is a universally popular sport supported by royalty, academics and common people alike, I can't bring myself to enjoy it. I was brought up in the country where we had dogs and hawks for hunting and I can't understand this obsession of Londoners with sports that cause one animal to rip another apart with no objective in mind. I hide my opinions lest people believe I'm a little strange.

The following day is the 14th. Many people are out to watch Northumberland's army leave for Norfolk but there are no cries of support, no cheering from the people along the way. Jane fears an uprising while the Duke is absent and orders the gates of the city to be guarded. She imposes a night time curfew inside the city.

Inside the Tower there's an almost unearthly silence now as the counsellors and courtiers sit and wait. Amy and I leave early to avoid being outside during the hours of curfew.

For the next two days the news is just as bad as it could be. Closer to London the people of Buckinghamshire have declared for Queen Mary. Jane is furious and has promised that all traitors will suffer their rightful punishment. The news from the east is even worse. At Framlingham in Suffolk Mary has been inspecting her troops and many of the towns in Norfolk that Robert had rallied to Jane's cause have now gone over to Mary. But there's worse to come. News arrives that the crews of five royal ships have mutinied off the coast of Norfolk and have gone over to Mary's side.

Inside the chambers of the royal court people say that Jane is sick. She's complaining that the skin is peeling from her back and blames the evil air in the Tower. But she's still working furiously, writing and signing letters to sheriffs and justices of the peace to demand that they deal with any subversion. And now it seems that there's disloyalty within the Tower as well as outside as some members of the Privy Council begin to murmur that all is lost and that Jane's cause should be abandoned.

Now Jane trusts no one. She orders a strong guard to be mounted around the Tower. When Amy and I try to leave that evening we find the gates locked.

"Open the gates this instance and let us through," demands Amy imperiously. The guard can see from our clothes that we are high ranking gentlewomen but it makes no difference.

"I'm sorry, my lady, but the gates are now closed until tomorrow by order of the Queen."

"Do you know who I am?" says Amy heatedly. "I am the daughter-in-law of the Duke. Bring the key immediately."

But the guard can't do this. Jane has the key and has taken it to bed with her!

We stand on the green discussing our next move and two young men approach us.

"Do you need a chamber for the night, ladies? We have fine chambers and you are very welcome to share them with us."

"Go to the devil," says Amy. "I'd rather sleep here on the green with my head on the block."

"You may yet do that," say the impudent pair laughing. "Good night ladies." They bow and walk away. Another figure is walking towards us. It's Mary Sidney and she's crying.

"Oh Mary. What's the matter?" I ask.

"It's father," she says. "There are some scandalous rumours going round court to blacken his name. Some are saying that he's been plotting with the French to put Mary, Queen of Scots, on the throne. Others say that he plans to give away English towns in France to gain French support and there's worse still. People are whispering that he's made Jane ill by poisoning her just as he did with Edward."

We're speechless. How can they say that? Moreover *who* is saying that?

"And Henry," says Mary referring to her husband, "Says that the situation is turning nasty and I'm to return home at once but now I can't go because the doors are locked. He'll think me disloyal and disobedient."

"I'm sure he won't think that, Mary," I say. "Don't worry, we'll vouch for you. We're in the same position and can't return home either."

"I have a chamber here," says Mary. "You're both welcome to share it with me."

So that's what we do. The three of us retire to Mary's small bed chamber, strip down to our shifts and share the very small bed where our proximity to each other, though hot, is most comforting - even though the smell of the Tower is pungent and even though, despite Amy's efforts to squash as many bugs as possible before we get into bed, we spend a night being eaten alive!

Chapter Seven
Saving our Skins

The next day we're up early, dressed and waiting for the Tower gates to be unlocked, which means waiting for Jane to arise since she has the key. Once outside we part company with Mary and thank her for her kindness. She's returning to her husband, Henry Sidney, and we're to await his instructions at Somerset House.

"Please take Henry's advice," says Mary. "On no account return to the Tower." She lowers her voice and whispers. "Henry believes Jane's cause is lost and cannot be revived. Mary has too much support now around the country and in the city itself. The situation's been handled badly and won't improve."

"What about Robert and his brothers?" asks Amy fearfully.

"Henry will do what he can when the time arrives," says Mary. "He's tried to distance himself from the plot for this reason, not out of disloyalty to us but because he can do little good if he's executed too."

'Executed too' – the words run round my brain. Clearly we have all to take care of ourselves. Who knows how Mary Tudor may decide to take revenge on the Dudley family.

"I'll keep you informed of any developments," says Mary, "And meanwhile stay inside and don't venture out."

Back in Somerset House we discuss what to do next. The servants bring us food but – is it my imagination? – they appear to be less willing to please and less talkative. Do they understand already that

we members of the Dudley family will be on the
losing side or are they simply mistrustful of everyone
at the moment? Only Mrs Picto, who looks after
Amy's gowns, behaves as she has always done. She
and Amy spend the time packing two wooden chests
with our clothing and rich cloths, taking care to pack
only what is ours and to leave everything that was in
the house when we arrived.

We didn't have to while away too much time. On
Wednesday 19th in the afternoon we hear the sound of
trumpets and a great cheering in the city followed by
the sound of church bells ringing everywhere. The
servants rush out of the house to join the crowds in
the streets and the smoke of many bonfires lit in
celebration rises above the houses. As darkness falls
the bonfires glow red in the night sky and still people
are celebrating.

We can guess what has happened. There's been
no war and the Privy Council has betrayed the Duke
and declared for the Princess Mary. That evening
Amy and I go down to the kitchen and prepare our
own supper. It's something we'll have to get used to
if we're lucky and escape imprisonment.

The following day we get our own breakfast. The
servants have returned but are still sleeping off the ale
from the previous night's celebrations and even Mrs
Picto's disappeared! Half way through the afternoon
Mary Sidney arrives. We exchange hugs and kisses.
Mary apologises for not coming earlier.

"Events moved so fast yesterday and took us all
by surprise," she says. She then explains how Jane's
father, the Duke of Suffolk, foolishly allowed the
Lord Mayor and members of the Privy Council to
leave the Tower for a supposed meeting with the

French Ambassador to plan for reinforcements to be sent to the Duke of Northumberland. But Suffolk had been tricked.

Instead the councillors met the Earl of Pembroke and the Earl of Arundel at Baynard's Castle, Pembroke's home in London. From there they proceeded to Cheapside in the city where they made the proclamation that Mary was now Queen. By the time they reached St Paul's the crowds of cheering people were so thick they could hardly pass through. Back in the Tower Jane's father was forced to sign the proclamation for Mary and announce it on Tower Hill. He then broke the news to his daughter who sadly left the throne room and the panoply of state and retired to the royal chambers.

The news this morning is that Jane's parents, the Duke and Duchess of Suffolk, have left the Tower for Pembroke's home to make an appeal for clemency for their family. Mary Sidney is fearful that they will claim, as will the other members of the Privy Council, they were all coerced into the plot by her father and that Northumberland will pay the price.

"So where is Jane now?" asks Amy.

"She's been removed from the royal apartments and is under arrest in a small house within the Tower," says Mary.

"And Guildford?"

"He's imprisoned in the Beauchamp Tower. The Duchess, our mother, is also under arrest. I'm afraid our kin will pay the price for all of this."

"Is there any news of Robert or the Duke?"

"The Earl of Arundel has set off with a large force to arrest the Duke, Ambrose, John and Henry. We have no news of Robert."

"Maybe he's escaped to France," says Amy hopefully.

"Maybe."

"What a scoundrel Arundel is," I say. "He pretended to support your father – he even said he was sorry he couldn't join him in the pursuit of Mary - and all the time he was scheming against him."

"Yes and so was Pembroke. And to make matters even worse Katherine Grey, Jane's sister, is married to the son of that treacherous old hypocrite. How must Katherine now feel? Her husband's father has betrayed her mother, father and sister!"

The three of us are silent as we reflect on the nasty business of politics.

Finally Mary says, "Henry has sent me to advise you to leave London at the earliest opportunity. We cannot offer you shelter as we have to appear to be unbiased for now and disconnect ourselves from my kin. Very soon Queen Mary will be back in the city and there will be an attempt to arrest all those implicated in the plot in any way, whether directly involved or not. Equally, when the servants realise the way the wind is blowing, they may well decide to betray you to Mary's men. You must leave quickly. Is there anyone you can trust?"

"There's James, Robert's groom."

"Pack up your things and ask James to take them to …."

"My mother's cousin has a small house in the city," says Amy.

"Well it's a start. Will she shelter you?"

"I expect so. I'll send James to ask her first."

"Do that this evening. Leave as soon as you can and tell no one where you're going." With this Mary wishes us 'God Speed' and takes her leave.

Amy goes in search of James but returns in despair. He's vanished into thin air.

"Go and find Picto, Kate," says Amy. "We'll just have to go and hope our cousins will take us in."

"But what about the clothes you packed? There's a cart in the stable."

"No that belongs to Elizabeth. We don't want to be accused of theft as well!"

Amy rummages in a small wooden box that she keeps locked and takes out some coins.

"I'll go down to the street to see if I can hire a cart and a driver," she says.

We go our separate ways but, while I come back with Mrs Picto, Amy returns still clutching her coins.

"They're either too drunk or too scared to help. No one's able to take us."

I can understand why. They could be accused of helping traitors to escape.

"We'll just have to leave without the chests. Maybe Elizabeth will have them sent on to us when she returns to Somerset House," says Amy.

Ha! From what I know of Elizabeth, Amy is dreaming! The princess has a reputation for acquisitiveness second to none and the dresses will go straight into her own collection, even if Amy were her best friend – which she clearly is not.

The three of us put some things into small bags that we can fasten to the saddles of our horses, clean shifts, fine woollen and linen stockings, combs and hoods decorated with pearls. Amy fastens a silk bag to her waist containing her jewellery and money.

In the stables are our two horses, two mules and another horse, a lovely mare, belonging to Robert. Valiant has gone with him into Norfolk. We can't take all of them and Mrs Picto will struggle to ride any of the horses.

"We'll saddle our two and a mule," decides Amy, "And we'll take the other mule to carry the bags."

"What about the mare? We can't leave her on her own."

But we have to. We can't lead Mrs Picto's mule and the baggage mule and manage the mare as well. Had Amy and I been better horse women it might be different.

The two of us set about saddling the horses and mule. When this is done we find a man's saddle for the second mule and fasten the bags securely onto this. But, as Amy goes to find some hay for the little mare we're leaving behind, she uncovers a heap of rags on the ground. Imagine her surprise when the rags give a loud snore!

"James, you lazy dog," she says kicking the rags with her toe, "Get up straight away. It's nearly evening."

James struggles uncertainly to his feet. He's obviously been sleeping off the effects of last night's ale. Amy grabs him by his collar and pushes his head into the horse trough outside.

"Waken up!"

Unsteadily James begins to saddle Robert's mare. Amy holds her while he hoists himself into the saddle. He's staggering on the ground but, once on the horse, he can ride as well as anyone. I then help Amy onto her horse and she takes the lead reins of the two mules, one on each side, while I help Mrs Picto into the saddle of one of them. Then I climb the mounting block and attempt to get on my horse unaided. James, who's now coming to his senses a little, rides alongside and steadies her.

Once I'm safely in the saddle, James takes the lead rope for Mrs Picto's mule and we set off for Amy's cousin's house. Outside the gate we stop and take a last look back at Somerset House. We've lived in this palace for six months and we won't see it again, ever. Our lives have changed irretrievably, we have no home and no idea what lies ahead.

When we arrive at our destination there are looks of astonishment and disapproval. Amy's cousin is much older than we are and scowls at us in a most unwelcoming manner. "Word gets around! She wasn't like this when I had the most powerful man in England for a father-in-law," remarks Amy grimly as we help James take the bags from the mule. A manservant comes out of the house and he and James lead the horses and mules to the mews round the corner. He'll sleep in the straw in the hayloft over the stable and the manservant takes him a bowl of pottage to eat.

The wooden and clay house is tiny compared to what we've been used to. Mrs Picto goes to join the two servants in the kitchen and, as the rest of the family have had their supper, Amy and I sit at the table to a bowl of mutton in a broth and some bread on a wooden platter. The bread is the coarse kind mixed with rye rather than the fine, sweet manchet bread we are used to and we are served ale instead of wine. Amy does not ask for sugar!

We eat everything we're given and are grateful. We have no idea when the next meal will be served and I have a strong suspicion that we've just eaten the finest in the house despite the homeliness of the fare and the icy welcome we received. The parents sit at the table and watch us eat, stony-faced, while their son and daughter, a little younger than we are, stand and watch, overawed by our fine clothes.

After the meal Amy thanks them kindly and asks if we may stay the night. Humility does not come naturally to her but now she must be humble. Unsmilingly the cousins agree and we're shown upstairs to a chamber that's clearly just been vacated by their daughter. The bed appears to have been slept in many times but we're grateful anyway.

"It's better than the Tower," says Amy when we're alone.

I'm wondering what will happen to Jane and Guildford now. Northumberland is as good as dead, that's a certainty, and I fear for all his sons though I cannot voice my fears to Amy whose face is pale and pinched with worry for Robert. As for the two of us - we are now homeless.

Chapter Eight
Retribution

The following morning I'm lying awake, and wondering whether Amy is too, when a voice says, "We'll go to William Hyde's house at Throcking. He's a loyal friend of Robert. He'll help us."

We sit with Amy's cousins and eat our breakfast in silence while James and the servant saddle the horses and mules. We won't be travelling at any pace faster than a walk so we eat our fill and forget the niceties of pretending we're not hungry. The next meal may be this evening.

After the usual courtesies we mount our horses and leave, riding for most of the morning up the road to the north, skirting the city and leaving it far behind. By early afternoon it's clear that Mrs Picto can travel no further.

"Are you unwell?" Amy asks her and the poor woman tells us that she's spent the previous night sleeping in a chair.

"What? They didn't find you a bed?" says Amy, incredulous and furious at the same time.

At the next inn we make a stop and James comes out with the good news that we can have chambers for the night.

Good news indeed! A more flea ridden place I've yet to find! In the morning we're all glad to be leaving it far behind. A good dinner at a hostelry at midday puts us in a better mood but I can see Amy counting the coins in her purse when she thinks no one's looking. I look down at my mother's brooch pinned at the top of my bodice and prepare myself to say goodbye to it.

That night we reach Ware, find good lodgings and are much cheered. Unfortunately Amy is ill the next day and has to stay in her chamber. We spend another night there but by midday she's well enough to travel again. Throcking is just to the west of Bury St Edmunds and we want to be at Hyde's house by evening.

But as we prepare to set off there's a huge commotion outside. A column of soldiers and horsemen are coming down the road from Cambridge to the north and we rush to the roadside to see them pass. At the head of the procession is the Earl of Arundel and who should be behind him but Northumberland, clearly discernable in his red cloak. Behind the Duke, mounted on their horses, are John, Ambrose and Henry, Amy's brothers-in-law. Young Henry is only sixteen; he looks terrified and is weeping. They are all surrounded by armed foot soldiers.

The people of the village jeer at Northumberland as he passes by and there are shouts of "Traitor!" and "Death to the enemies of Queen Mary!" Our manner of dress marks us out from the crowd and I rather think that Ambrose sees us as they ride past for he gives a faint smile. But he doesn't acknowledge us, knowing the danger that may place us in. Amy scans the procession for Robert but he's not with them.

Subdued and silent we mount our horses and head north in the opposite direction. By late afternoon we're in Throcking.

The reception at William Hyde's house is so different from the one we had in London at Amy's cousins.

"My dear Amy, you look so pale and ill. You are welcome here. Come inside, come inside." Amy bursts into tears and sobs with relief and self pity. Once inside and fortified by a glass of spiced wine, she begs for news of Robert but William and his wife are unable to help. We then exchange our news from London with William's from Cambridge.

It seems that the Duke left Bury St Edmunds when he received news of the Council's treachery. His recruits had begun to desert him and he fled to Cambridge where he thought he would receive a sympathetic reception, pleading that he had only been carrying out Edward's wishes. He had thrown his hat in the air, feigning joy at the proclamation that Mary was Queen. But his dissembling didn't impress anyone and he was detained by the city magistrates. Then Arundel arrived and arrested him with his sons but Robert was not with the other brothers. This story tallies with what we saw at the roadside outside the inn at Ware.

The next day William Hyde sends one of his men to London to find out the latest news. We'll have to wait several days now and spend the time with Mrs Picto attending to what's left of our possessions. Mrs Hyde has given us two of her old gowns and some material out of which we hope to fashion new gowns and kirtles. Mrs Picto is an expert needlewoman and, though the material is plain and unfashionable, at least we will have a change of dress. Our best clothes can be put away for special occasions.

On 6th August William's man returns. The news is both good and bad. Elizabeth, having heard the proclamations of Mary's victory, had ridden from Hatfield where she'd been lying low. Together with a great retinue of followers she went out to greet Mary as she rode in triumph into London. The two sisters had put on an unrivalled show of splendour and unity as they entered the city to the cheers of the crowds.

"Trust Elizabeth to come out of the woodwork and emerge on the winning side," says Amy sarcastically.

More importantly as far as Amy is concerned is the news that Robert is alive, having been taken prisoner in King's Lynn and then to Framlingham Castle in Suffolk. He's now with his father and brothers in the Tower. William Hyde's man has discovered that Mary does not wish to begin her reign with violence and recrimination. She will execute only the ring leaders after they have been tried for treason and will pardon where she can.

As far as Northumberland's sons are concerned, this sends a mixed message. Certainly the Duke is doomed but how many others? We will have to wait and see.

"What of the Sidneys? Have you heard anything?" asks Amy.

But the man has heard nothing. Only that Queen Mary has freed the Duke of Suffolk, Jane's father, at the Duchess' request. When we reflect how Jane once insulted Lady Mary with great arrogance over Mary's religious beliefs we're amazed at this. We can only assume that Suffolk has pleaded coercion by Northumberland. It's obvious who will pay the price.

So we have no choice other than to sit, sew and wait for news. William Hyde and his wife are great friends of Robert and are most kind; Amy and I are very comfortable at Throcking. She writes to her

parents in Norfolk to tell them of our situation and
well being and her father replies affectionately.

By late August there has been a flurry of letters
and the news from London is grim. Amy's father-in-
law, together with John Gates and Thomas Palmer,
who rode out with the Duke to fight Mary's forces,
have all been executed for treason.

Northumberland had tried to plead for his life and
even gave up his evangelical religion in an attempt to
show his contrition. He worshipped in the Catholic
fashion by attending mass and made a public
declaration stating that he had been wrong in his
beliefs. He also apologised for his role in the Duke of
Somerset's downfall and begged forgiveness of
Somerset's sons. Even to the end he'd hoped he
would be reprieved especially when his execution
was postponed for a day.

But Mary had delayed merely to emphasise the
huge moral victory she had achieved; the message
was that evangelicals were not so sure of their faith
that they were prepared to die for it! The following
day Northumberland, Gates and Palmer said mass in
the chapel in the Tower and then were taken to Tower
Hill to be executed. It was reported to us that
Northumberland had then hinted darkly at another
person who had been the leader of the plot to put Jane
on the throne but the Duke refused to name him. Had
he meant Gates, we wonder, or perhaps Suffolk
himself? One thing is certain. We will never know;
only that these three men took the punishment for
many guilty people on the Privy Council.

A huge crowd numbering thousands had gathered
for the executions apparently and the unpopular
Northumberland had gone to the block first to the

delight of them all. He had been beheaded with one stroke of the axe but Gates had not been so fortunate; it took three strokes to remove his head. By the time it was Palmer's turn, the elderly man had skipped up the steps of the scaffold, confessed to his part in Somerset's downfall and had stated, almost joyfully, his belief in the forgiveness of God and his willingness to die. He showed no fear despite the gory sight of the blood splattered executioner and the scaffold, already soaked with the blood of Northumberland and Gates, and his end was mercifully quick. Once the three executions had been carried out, the crowd had dispersed; the entertainment was over.

William Hyde reads the letter quietly and by the time he reaches the end, we are all too shocked to say a word. We sit and reflect, in our thoughts and our own private prayers, our concerns for the unfortunate young men who still await their fates. In truth Northumberland had been fortunate. A traitor's death would have been far worse.

Eventually, after a long silence, William speaks. We are not to be downhearted for Robert, he says; the young man has courage and it's a good sign that Mary has not yet executed other rebels. She seems to be showing compassion and leniency. And the Duke had pleaded for mercy for his sons before he died, Amy says hopefully. Also, she adds, John, the eldest brother, who's been convicted of treason along with his father, has been spared execution – at least, so far.

We all agree. Queen Mary has achieved a major coup for her Catholic faith by persuading Northumberland to change his beliefs, giving him false hope that he would be pardoned. It has demonstrated very well how weak we evangelicals are in our faith. Perhaps she will be content with that.

Amy and I retire to the chapel to pray for Robert and his brothers. There's no need to pray for the souls of those who have died; unlike the Catholics, we believe that simply dying in faith is sufficient to send us to heaven. We remember Jane in our prayers for, it is said that, while she has comfortable lodgings in the Tower, the guards now make fun of her. Poor, proud Jane, how she will feel the insults! We also remember Katherine, her sister.

Jane's sister, Katherine, is only thirteen and was married at the same time as Jane at the magnificent triple wedding. To think that was just three months ago at Durham Place and how quickly everything has changed! Katherine, so unlike her sister, lively, full of fun and incredibly pretty, and her equally young husband were said to be very fond of each other but, last week in a letter from Mary Sidney, we discovered that they too have been touched by this tragedy.

Katherine's father-in-law, the treacherous Pembroke who betrayed her whole family, has now lost no time arranging for a divorce for his son. The young couple are said to be heartbroken. Katherine is back with her parents, the recently pardoned Duke and Duchess of Suffolk.

"We'll lose all our property and titles," says Amy, "Since father-in-law was a convicted traitor."

"Well Robert hasn't been attainted yet," I say, "So I don't think we can jump to conclusions. Surely it's only the Duchess of Northumberland who will lose the houses that her husband owned."

"Robert hasn't been tried for treason yet but he will be; I'm certain of it, Kate. What will we do?

Where will we live? We will be as penniless as the poorest beggars. We can't live on Mr Hyde's charity forever."

It's a gloomy thought. To go home to Stanfield House will be our only course of action and one that I know Amy will be reluctant to take. Her half brothers and sisters were all older and, as the baby of the family, she was quite spoiled. Her father had been so proud of her when she and Robert were married at Sheen Palace in the presence of the King. How could she now go back, penniless and degraded to be shamed in front of them all? At night, safe in the privacy of her chamber, I hear her sobs.

Chapter Nine
London

The time passes and a weariness sets in. Amy never
smiles and her face is lined with a worried frown.
Then we receive letters from Mary Sidney which
provide the faint glimmers of hope. It seems that
Mary's husband, Henry Sidney, and the former
Duchess of Northumberland, her mother, are doing all
they can to persuade Queen Mary to be lenient
towards Robert and his brothers in the Tower. Sir
Henry Sidney has sisters who are favourites of the
Queen and this has allowed him to escape retribution
despite his marriage to a Dudley girl.

Mary Sidney says that the Queen is more than
willing to take advice from her cousin, Charles V,
Holy Roman Emperor, and his son, Prince Philip, of
Spain. So it has been towards Spain that Henry
Sidney has turned for help. And to Amy's great joy
the Spanish nobles are making representations to
Queen Mary on our behalf.

Amy sits down immediately to reply; it will take
her all afternoon to compose a letter and to choose the
right words, words that do not imply any conspiracy
or double meaning, words that cannot implicate her in
any plotting and result in her own imprisonment.
Letters can be intercepted by the vast network of
spies who lie in every county; it pays to be careful.

In the past Robert had admired Elizabeth for her
ability to use high flown phrases and biblical
quotations in her attempts, usually successful, to
cover up her true meaning or message of support to a
scheming courtier. Amy had despised Elizabeth's
cunning but now she has to use similar tactics herself.

She asks William Hyde to read the letter before she hands it to the courier. William suggests she scores lines through the spaces where there is no writing. In this way no incriminating sentences can be added.

Amy is now more optimistic and happier than she has been for ages. A week later eighteen yards of woollen cloth arrive from Norfolk, a gift from the estates of her father and, with winter coming, no present could have been so well received. Mrs Hyde, Mrs Picto, Amy and I, assisted by two of Mrs Hyde's women get to work cutting out and sewing new shifts for the cold weather.

As September progresses the fruit in the garden and park has to be harvested and made into preserves. Mr Hyde encourages us to get out in the fresh air and help the servants and, although we haven't done this since we were children in Norfolk, we find ourselves enjoying the harvest and the simple picnics outdoors. We borrow linen aprons and over gowns from the servants and fill baskets with plums, blackberries, quince and apples. Back inside the kitchen we turn them into the most heavenly preserves for winter delicacies and Amy, with her love of all things sweet, is in her own true kingdom.

"I have to taste this to make sure it's just right," she says, helping herself liberally to a piece of bread and quince jelly, while the servants laugh.

One day at the end of September, while we're standing beneath an apple tree holding our aprons to catch the apples thrown down by the servant boy, a rider on a sweating, foam-flecked horse comes up the drive. He has a letter for a 'Lady Amy Dudley'. You can see his surprise and disbelief when he discovers that the woman standing before him, golden curls tied back under a simple linen bonnet, is the 'Lady' in question. Amy's hand shakes as she takes the letter from him.

She scans the letter line by line and then goes back to the top to read it again. Finally her hands drop to her sides and she looks at me in disbelief.

"Is the news good ….. ?" My voice fades away.

"It's good," she says, breathlessly, "It's very good. It's from the Sidneys. Mary tells me that I can visit Robert in the Tower. The Spaniards at court have persuaded the Queen to allow all the Dudley wives to visit their husbands provided we obtain the Lieutenant's permission before each visit."

To the surprise of the messenger, we fling our arms around each other and dance around before running inside to tell everyone.

The next few days are spent running about trying to make preparations. The messenger is sent back to Mary Sidney with the usual carefully worded reply in case it's intercepted. Amy's learning something of Elizabeth's guile as she invokes the Biblical story of Ruth and thanks 'our most gracious sovereign Lady, Queen Mary, for her abundant kindness to her children, the people; just as Ruth cared for her kinswoman, Naomi, so does she show her love for each and every one of us,' and so on in that same flattering (and in no way blameworthy) style. The letter also asks Mary Sidney if she can find us suitable lodgings in the city close to the Tower. William Hyde has already said that he will help us with a loan of money in that respect.

In the end we have no need of Mr Hyde's generous offer. Although Mary has herself been attainted and stripped of any land or titles, her husband, Henry Sidney, has been allowed to keep his title and property and we're invited to join them at their house in London and afterwards in Kent, where Henry and Mary live with Henry's aging and infirm father at the magnificent castle called Penshurst Place.

The Sidneys are the only members of the family who are still very wealthy. Queen Mary seems to look favourably upon Henry Sidney and it would seem Henry's sisters and the Spanish nobles are largely responsible for this.

A few days later Amy, Mrs Picto, James and I are back on the road to London once again. Amy's only sadness is that she's not been able to visit her dear father, Sir John, before winter as she'd planned. Now it will have to wait until the spring as the roads will soon be impassable when the bad November weather begins.

William Hyde has allowed us to have the use of a small cart to which James harnesses the mules. Our new clothing chests and Mrs Picto will travel in it and James will drive. Amy and I will ride alongside on our horses while Robert's mare will remain with Mr and Mrs Hyde at Throcking. Amy and I put, in the larger of the two wooden chests, our two finest gowns, kirtles, French hoods, jewellery and velvet embroidered slippers together with the two gowns Mrs Hyde gave us and our new woollen shifts and stockings. Mrs Picto puts her second gown and shift into the small chest; with them she folds a woollen shirt and breeches for James who also has a new pair of leather shoes courtesy of the kind Mr Hyde.

Thanks to our industry during the past few weeks, we three women all wear new gowns and kirtles; it's true that these are plainer than Amy and I have been accustomed to but this will help to protect us from thieves on the journey. We no longer look like wealthy people travelling to London.

Amy and I hug and kiss the kind people who have been our friends for the past two months and who have done so much for us. Then we're lifted into the saddle by Mr Hyde's servants. It's the first time we've used our leather buskin boots and riding gloves since we arrived, ill and friendless, in July and we're leaving with so much more than the few possessions we brought. At the last moment Mrs Hyde laughs and puts four earthenware jars of preserves into the cart, cider for the journey and a basket of apples.

"One jar of preserve for you and your family, Amy," says Mrs Hyde, meaning for all four of us, "One for Mary and Henry and two for dearest Robert and the boys, if the Lieutenant will allow you to take food into the Tower. God speed."

They watch our little train depart down the drive and, looking back, we see them wave goodbye and suddenly feel very sad to be leaving this peaceful place. What a contrast London will be. The little cart rumbles along the road and the weather is kind to us. Amy uses the money Mr Hyde has given her to pay for a night's lodging at the little inn at Ware and how they stare when they perceive our changed circumstances from our homely dress! But our money is as good as ever! Amy and I collapse in fits of laughter when we're in our chamber.

As we amble along the road the next day, Amy says, "I wonder what's happened to the chests of fine clothes we left behind at Somerset House."

"Shall we send James to make enquiries when we reach the city?" I ask. "It's worth trying."

"No," replies Amy, shaking her head, "They'll be at Hatfield by now. We all know what Elizabeth's like. If ever we meet again, we'll probably see her wearing them – or one of her gentlewomen! Of course they'll have to let them out first."

At that rather stinging, and of course completely untrue, insinuation about Elizabeth's girth, we're both racked with fits of laughter again, so much so that James and Mrs Picto turn round in puzzlement.

"Maybe we should take a deviation from our path and call at Hatfield House to ask if we can have our clothes back," I remark. More laughter and Mrs Picto tut-tuts and shakes her head! But we all know that Elizabeth's acquisitive nature is legendary. I can just imagine her face when she found two trunks of gorgeous gowns abandoned at Somerset House. She would not have taken any trouble to try to discover where their owner was, especially when she realised that they were Amy's!

We're able to travel for a full day with a break at an inn for dinner. Mrs Picto is happy in the little cart and we're proceeding slowly and comfortably. Every little while we stop by a stream to give the horses and mules a drink and allow them a snatch of grass. It's good to stretch our legs too and have cider from the large jug Mrs Picto guards, or an apple and a sweet cake. The sun is shining but every so often a cold gust of wind reminds us that autumn is here. Everywhere there are people working on the fields, hurrying to get in the harvest before the weather changes. Overhead wild geese and ducks are, like us, flying to their winter homes. It's a pleasant landscape.

By evening we're in London in the house that the Sidneys own. Mary and Henry are not at home but the servants are expecting us and welcome us inside - they regard our manner of dress with curiosity! After our progress through the countryside London seems dirty and the smell is overpowering but the Sidney's house, like all large houses, is a haven away from the bustle of the city. We have to get used to the routine of life in the city again.

At the beginning of October Mary and Henry return to their London home. Lady Dudley, the tainted former Duchess of Northumberland, is with them and we are shocked by her appearance. Her face is lined and grey and her posture stooped and dispirited; she now looks like a very old lady. Amy and I greet her with a deep curtsey.

"So you are to visit Robert," says Lady Dudley to Amy, "Anne, Elizabeth and Margaret have already visited their husbands."

Amy looks down at the ground at this obvious reprimand and says nothing. Lady Dudley's making sure that Amy knows she's neglecting her wifely duties.

"That's hardly fair, mother," says Mary. "For one thing Amy doesn't have her own private fortune as does Elizabeth Tailboys, Ambrose's wife, and her kin do not own a large enough house in the city. She's been forced to depend upon the charity of friends in Hertfordshire. Had she returned to her mother's house she would have been even further away. She's done as much as she could under the circumstances."

"And I asked her to wait until I returned from Penshurst so that I could escort her to the Tower," says Henry.

Amy gives them both a grateful look and Lady Dudley gives a faint half smile, or was it a sneer! Amy is not her favourite daughter-in-law due to her lack of fortune and relatively lowly birth and she'd not been too pleased with Robert for making such a poor match. Inwardly I sigh; will the Dudleys ever cease to be ambitious? Even now with all the family either convicted of treason or awaiting trial, she cannot forget her towering ambition.

Before any more cutting remarks can be made the servants arrive to announce supper. Later we play cards by candlelight; the nights are drawing in now, reminding us that it will soon be cold enough to light a fire. Back in Amy's bed chamber she complains about her mother-in-law.

"She's always disliked me because Robert married me for love and not for fortune. And another thing, Elizabeth Lady Tailboys, Ambrose's wife, has a lot of property of her own in Lincolnshire and Yorkshire and Henry's wife, Margaret, is a rich heiress too. Even Anne, John's wife, is a Seymour and has wealthy kin to help her."

"Well try not to feel too angry, Amy," I say, "And remember that they've all suffered misfortune too. Ambrose has Elizabeth now but he lost his first wife due to the sweating sickness little more than a year ago and his baby daughter too. Henry's wife, Margaret Audley, will lose her huge fortune to the crown when Henry's attainted and poor Anne Seymour, John's wife, saw her father, Somerset, executed on trumped up charges due, in part, to her father-in-law, Northumberland! How must that have made her feel about the man *she* married?"

Amy nods. It's a sobering thought that John Dudley, the eldest son, had seen his own father send his wife's father to his death over a year ago. Northumberland had confessed from the scaffold to his part in the conviction of an innocent man, something he bitterly regretted in the face of death.

"And think of poor Guildford. At eighteen he's separated from his wife Jane and stands little chance of ever seeing her again."

"What will happen to us all?" says Amy, shaking her head. It's not a question that I'd like to answer. Little wonder, I think, that women these days suffer so much from depression with their scheming and ambitious husbands.

The following morning however Amy's in good spirits as she sets off with Henry Sidney for the Tower. Henry has already obtained permission from the Lord Lieutenant for her visit and her only problem now is what she should wear! She wants Robert to see her at her best so she chooses the fine gown and velvet kirtle she wore when we left Somerset House in such a hurry in July. She chooses her best French hood with the pearls and embroidery but has to wear her leather riding boots as the day promises to be wet and the paths between the house and the boat jetty will be muddy. With a cloak borrowed from Mary she looks quite the lady once again.

As she's going through the door she remembers the two jars of preserve that Mrs Hyde gave her when we left Throcking. A servant brings them in a basket.

While she's away Mary sends one of Henry's men to Somerset House to enquire about our two hastily abandoned chests of clothes. Elizabeth's servants declare they know nothing of them and say that they must have been stolen by persons unknown during the period of unrest after Jane declared herself Queen!

Chapter Ten
Protestation and Unrest

Amy and Henry are back home by late afternoon. Amy is considerably excited and her cheeks are flushed.

"The Lieutenant of the Tower was so kind. He smiled at me and showed me to a bed chamber where Robert and I could be together and all alone. He left us there and went to dine with Henry. It was wonderful, Kate. Robert's in good spirits and we had a whole afternoon together." She gives me a meaningful look and smiles broadly when she says this.

"Robert's sharing chambers with Guildford in the Bell Tower but Guildford is sad because he's not allowed to see Jane. She's in a small cottage within the Tower but she's not allowed outside even though the boys can walk out on the leads. John, Ambrose and Henry are in the Beauchamp Tower. Robert says that the main problem is boredom. They carve on the wooden tables and chests and even on the stone walls, Robert says."

Amy's face then falls and she looks troubled. "Jane and Guildford are awaiting trial. Queen Mary was willing to pardon them all after Northumberland's execution but Bishop Gardiner and Ambassador Renard are attempting to influence the Queen to punish them. Who knows what that will mean!"

"Don't worry, Amy," I remark, desperately trying to think of something optimistic to say, "Nothing has happened yet and there's been plenty of opportunity for the Queen to exact vengeance. We have to trust in our Lord Jesus to stand by their side and watch over them."

But unfortunately they need more than the help of the Lord.

Bishop Gardiner's been pressing for rapid religious changes in church and this has taken the people in the city by surprise. Services are now conducted in Latin as they were ten years ago and the altars are decorated with silver crosses and candles once more. The ritual of worship has been restored and the mass has replaced the evangelical form of communion. Now the bread or host is raised to heaven by the priest at the moment it is transformed into the body of Christ. Even the evangelicals, who had recognised Mary's right to the throne, have been shocked by the swift reversal of religious practice and there is a growing voice of dissent in the city. Printed pamphlets opposing the changes have been distributed in the city and a dead dog with a shaved head like a monk has been flung through a window into a meeting of the Queen and her Council, much to Queen Mary's anger and revulsion.

Even worse there are rumours that the Queen intends to make a marriage with the Hapsburgs and, unbelievably, the name of her young cousin, Prince Philip of Spain, has been mentioned. Henry Sidney has all the news from court and intends to use his knowledge to save Robert and his brothers if he can. Already he's friendly with Renard and other Spaniards at court.

"But the Queen's practically an old lady," says Amy one evening at supper, "And Prince Philip is still in his twenties. Why would he want to marry her?"

"Well Queen Mary is thirty seven and could still have a child. Philip is twenty six. There's an eleven year gap. Not insurmountable. And Philip will have to do whatever his father, the Holy Roman Emperor, tells him," says Henry Sidney.

"You would do well to hold your tongue and keep your opinions to yourself," says Lady Dudley to Amy, "Otherwise you will undo all the good work that Henry and I have done to secure the boys' release."

But as the weeks progress it's obvious that the protesters in London don't intend to keep their opinions to themselves. Every day there's news of another disturbance, another gathering of dissatisfied and mistrustful citizens. Despite the Queen's reassurances that any marriage she makes abroad would never result in England becoming part of the Hapsburg Empire, the people are not convinced and alarm spreads rapidly.

Even worse for our family, Gardiner has convinced the Queen to bring Jane and Guildford to trial, together with the old Archbishop, Cranmer, who is imprisoned in the Tower with them. Ambrose and young Henry Dudley are to be tried at the same time. This is not a good sign. Trials for treason are usually forgone conclusions.

On a cold November day a procession leaves the Tower and winds its way towards Westminster Hall. Amy and I join the crowds along the route. Jane is dressed all in black and carries her prayer book open before her. Another prayer book hangs from her waist. Guilford, who precedes her with Cranmer, is likewise dressed in black; his velvet sleeves are slashed to reveal a white satin lining beneath. At sixteen and eighteen they look such a pathetically young couple. Ambrose and Henry follow behind.

The crowd is silent as they pass by. No one wanted this. We wait to see what will happen but, when they return, the yeoman leading the procession has turned his axe inwards, a voiceless statement of the guilty verdict. Jane is condemned to be burned alive and the men to suffer the hideous deaths of traitors, to be hanged by the neck, cut down while still alive, disembowelled and their privy parts removed, before they are finally beheaded and quartered. Jane and Guildford are composed as they walk by but women weep at the sight of them.

"Take heart in this," I say to Amy as we walk home, "Henry Sidney says that Queen Mary doesn't want any more executions and he's doing all he can to gain the support of the Spaniards."

"Let's hope Prince Philip will have the old bat," says Amy, looking over her shoulder to make sure no one's within ear shot, "That should sweeten her up."

Christmas approaches and during Advent Jane is allowed to take exercise on the green outside her lodgings in the Tower. It's a good sign and Robert tells Amy that Guildford can see his wife sometimes from the leads. He's desperate to talk to her again.

Henry Sidney, of necessity, must spend Christmas at court so we remain at home with Mary and Lady Dudley. It's a quiet time with none of the usual jollities of the season. We have our Christmas feasts but can hardly enjoy them for thinking of the poor prisoners in the Tower. Still the servants expect to enjoy the rich food that's sent down from the top table and Lady Dudley is adamant that there should be enough remaining to feed the poor who gather

97

outside. This year there's plenty of rejected food to go round; our appetites are dulled.

In the New Year the Spanish delegation comes in force through the city. It's rumoured that they are here to sign the marriage treaty and, despite a heavy snowfall, people turn out in great numbers to see these dark haired and strangely dressed foreigners. The Spaniards wave regally and in a gentile manner to the crowds but small boys pelt them with snowballs in return. The people go home sorrowfully, shaking their heads with doubt for the future.

In mid-January, however, comes even more frightening news. In addition to the mounting tide of rebellion in the city over the question of the Spanish marriage, there are reports of an uprising in the West Country and the Welsh Marches. It's even said that Jane's father, the Duke of Suffolk, is trying to raise an army in the Midlands. As January progresses the mood of revolt spreads and the Queen begins to recruit troops to defend the city. By now it's rumoured that there are French ships assembling off the coast of Normandy awaiting their orders to invade England in support of the rebels.

By the end of January the rebellions in Devon, Wales and Leicestershire have failed for lack of support and Jane's father is in the Tower with his daughter once more. However, a knight named Thomas Wyatt has raised an enormous army in Kent and is marching on London from Maidstone. Mary's soldiers and five hundred Whitecoats from the city set out to meet them south of the Thames. When the two forces meet there is confusion and reluctance by many of the Whitecoats to fight Wyatt and his fellow

Englishmen in support of the Spaniards. Many defect to Wyatt's forces and what is left of Mary's army is seen by us on its return to London; their jackets are torn and worn inside out to prevent them from being arrested as deserters. They've lost their weapons and look very afraid.

Henry Sidney returns from the court at Westminster, breathless and in a state of agitation.

"We're asking the Queen to leave the city and go to the castle at Windsor," he says. "She'll have more protection there. We cannot be sure that, when the rebels enter the city, as they surely will, other people will not join them. They have a lot of support. Hastings and Cornwallis are negotiating with the rebels at Deptford and trying to work out a peaceful solution. It may be a good idea for everyone in this house to go to Penshurst where you will all be safe."

"And you? What will you do?" asks Mary.

"I will stay with the Queen of course. I must, Mary. It's my duty and a greater duty than I have even to you. Already the Queen is saying she will stay at Westminster and lead her forces herself if necessary."

"She can't do that. She's a woman; only a king can lead an army."

"I know and I fear for all of us. There's every chance that Wyatt will succeed. He intends to put Elizabeth on the throne."

"Elizabeth!" gasps Amy. "She's just as likely to marry a Spanish prince as her sister. Where will that get us? There'll be a civil war. I might have known that her name would appear in the plot somewhere!"

99

"Anyway," says Mary, "If you are staying in London, Henry, we'll wait here for you and that's the end of the matter. I won't leave you."

Lady Dudley is too shocked by the news to speak but I wonder if she's thinking what I'm thinking. If Wyatt is successful and Elizabeth is given the crown, the Dudley boys will most likely be spared. But it will probably be the end of Henry Sidney's career if he fights for Queen Mary. It's difficult to predict which side will win and who to support and the stakes are high. For Henry the matter is simple; he'll fight for the crown. He kisses Mary farewell and goes back to Whitehall Palace.

The Queen doesn't run away and by Candlemas, 2nd February, there's news that she's ridden out to meet her people, just as her father would have done, and has given such a rousing speech outside the Guildhall that everyone present began cheering and vouching their support. Mary has shown no fear and has instead chatted pleasantly and graciously to Londoners along the route passing by Fleet Street and through Ludgate.

Oh yes, Mary knows how to handle the crowds and has given them all the assurances they needed regarding the Spanish marriage. She will not marry Prince Philip, she says, without the full support of parliament and the Privy Council. By the time she's finished the crowd is cheering not only for the Queen but for Prince Philip too! The livery companies raise the men she needs and the city of London is armed and waiting.

From the highest points of the city Wyatt's army can be seen across the Thames in Southwark. Two large guns are trained on us from the southern end of

London Bridge which has its drawbridge lifted. Wyatt begins the bombardment of the bridge in the hope that the drawbridge will be lowered to let him in. We can now only sit and wait to see what will happen next.

On the 6th February, Shrove Tuesday, there are none of the usual celebrations before Lent begins. All London is quiet and the siege has stopped but, as we begin to hope for an end to the rebellion, there are rumours that Wyatt is looking for another place to cross the river.

In the early hours of the morning of Ash Wednesday we're awakened by a tremendous commotion. Wyatt and his men are in the city having crossed the river at Kingston during the night. The mood now is one of panic with people running down the streets screaming, "Get up and defend your city or you will all be murdered in your beds! Take up arms and assemble at Charing Cross." A soldier outside our home tells us that Wyatt's forces are gathered at Hyde Park and that the Queen is still at the Palace of Whitehall as far as he knows.

Mary's horrified. "Wyatt has a huge force of men. Everyone at Westminster will be slaughtered," she says. We've had no news of Henry since he came to ask us to flee to Kent. By daybreak there's a tumultuous uproar and the shouting of panic stricken voices everywhere. We retreat inside the house and bar the doors.

Throughout the morning there's the sound of fighting. We hear that a group of rebels has tried to enter the royal palace of Whitehall and that they moved on to Charing Cross when they found the gates were barred against them.

In the afternoon, apart from the occasional cannon shot, all is quiet. What in heaven's name is happening? We wait all afternoon before one of Henry's servants volunteers to go outside and find out what he can. When he returns we don't know whether to be fearful or rejoice. Wyatt has been arrested and the rebels are being rounded up and taken to the Tower. Considering the size of the rebellion there have been few deaths and the Queen is safe.

"Queen Mary will not be so forgiving this time. There will be many executions," says Mary Sidney, grimly.

The following day London has almost returned to normal apart from the fact that there are soldiers going from door to door, seeking the Whitecoat deserters who went over to Wyatt's side. On Friday a white faced Henry Sidney returns from court with appalling news.

"It was a close run thing," he says, "The guards outside the palace left closing the gates to the last minute and Wyatt's men were almost upon us. They could still have overtaken us but they were disorganised and divided. In the end they were defeated just up the road at Charing Cross. We were fortunate and I've never seen the Queen so angry."

Henry gulps hard and looks round to see if Mary's mother has come into the chamber. "Mary, I have some very bad news for you and I beg you not to tell your mother until we've had time to prepare her."

Mary looks at him aghast. We have no idea what he will say next but Amy and I exchange fearful glances.

"This rebellion will have all kinds of unforeseen effects," says Henry, staring at the ground. He cannot look Mary in the eye. "Bishop Gardiner has long been advising the Queen that she is too soft hearted with rebels and too eager to forgive," he continues. And we suddenly realise where this is leading.

"Gardiner's insisting that Jane and Guildford are the focus of dissent for those who scorn Catholicism and oppose the Spanish marriage. He's insisting on their immediate execution."

"But they had nothing to do with Wyatt," says Amy indignantly.

Mary Sidney is more resigned. She's expected this for some time.

"When?" she says quietly.

Chapter Eleven
Savage Executions

Three days later, the following Monday, 12th February, an eighteen year old youth, little more than a tall, slender boy, walks out of the Tower and climbs Tower Hill to face the gathered crowds. He is dignified and brave and the crowd is silent, shocked to see someone so young condemned to die. Mary has commuted his sentence to death by the axe; there will be no horrific quarterings.

Guildford stands tall on the scaffold and forgives the executioner. He has refused the services of a priest, denying Mary the moral victory she gained when his father was executed. The young man must be terrified but he does not show his fear; his tall figure, elegantly dressed in black velvet, is calm and proud as he removes his doublet and kneels before the block to make his last prayer. He is pathetic in his loneliness. A woman in the crowd sobs, the axe falls and the bloody body is dragged away to be brought back to the Tower in a cart, the head wrapped in a blood stained white cloth. The body is thrown unceremoniously into the vault of the chapel where his father had once prayed for his life.

Jane sees the returning cart and prepares to meet her own end on the green inside the Tower, away from the prying eyes and the sensation seekers of the crowd outside. She wears the same clothes as the ones she wore for her trial and carries the same prayer book. Jane is accompanied by the kindly and sympathetic priest with whom she's had many lively discussions over the previous days, refusing to budge in her convictions and eliciting a fatherly admiration in the sorrowful man.

The assembled crowd of nobles, ambassadors and churchmen listen in silence as Jane addresses them bravely. She intends to die a martyr. Her lady in waiting helps her to remove her bodice and then Jane falters, asking the axe man whether he will administer the blow before she is ready. He replies that he will not and, reassured, she fastens the blindfold and drops to her knees on the straw.

The lonely tiny figure then crawls over the straw to the horror of the onlookers, as she searches desperately for the block. Disorientated and not finding it where she imagined it to be, she calls for help. The surrounding courtiers are shocked to the core at this pathetic sight and a woman steps forward to guide Jane. Women weep as the girl who might once have been Queen says her last prayer and the axe falls. The Spanish ambassador later says that he would not have believed how one so small could produce so much blood. Her body joins that of her husband in the crypt under the Tower chapel, finally reunited in death.

Jane and Guildford had both written, in a prayer book, messages of strength and support to Jane's father, the Duke of Suffolk, who is awaiting his own execution. Guildford, who was a kindly young man, expressed his affection for his father in law.

Back at the Sidney's house we listen to the account of the execution in horror.

"Imagine how he must feel reading that and knowing that his support for the rebels has brought about his own daughter's death!" says Amy.

"Guildford may have forgiven Suffolk but I don't think mother ever will," says Mary.

"How is she today?"

"She cries incessantly. There's no consoling her and she keeps to her chamber and eats nothing. She will make herself ill. Nothing is more certain."

Henry walks into the chamber at this point and we're all talking at once asking for news of John, Robert, Ambrose and Henry. Surely Mary will not have them all executed.

"There's good news and bad," he says. "The Spanish ambassador has intimated that Philip wouldn't want the other brothers to be executed and this has stayed the Queen's hand for now - she doesn't wish to offend her future husband - but while this is good news it will mean that our family will have a debt of honour to Philip in the future."

"Debt of honour?" says Amy.

"They may be required to fight for Spain and the Emperor when Queen Mary marries Philip."

"Do you think she really will marry him after all this dissent?"

"Nothing more certain. She's made up her mind. But right now there are more pressing matters such as the execution of the rebels. Gallows are being erected at all the gates into the city. At the earliest opportunity I want you all to go to Penshurst away from the horrors that will shortly visit London."

But it isn't easy to leave the city. As Mary had predicted, her mother's made herself ill with grief over Guildford's death and we'll have to wait until she's well enough to travel. Even worse she's now convinced that the tragedy is all Robert's fault.

"Why? Why does she blame Lord Robert," I ask Mary when Amy's busy elsewhere.

"Grief is making her demented. She believes that Robert didn't do enough when father sent him to Norfolk to apprehend the fleeing Lady Mary and she says that, if Robert had captured Mary, we would now all be in different circumstances. In short, she holds him responsible for father's death and now for Guildford's."

"Does Robert know this?"

"I don't think so but Amy's beginning to feel her wrath and believes it's directed at her alone. She thinks it's a personal matter." Mary Sidney hesitates before continuing. "I don't know quite how to say this, Katherine, but it may be better if you and Amy went to live elsewhere until mother is better and restored to her proper mind."

"But where will we go? We're practically paupers and cannot expect Mr Hyde to keep us indefinitely."

"Amy's maternal grandfather, Mr Scott, has a house at Camberwell, Southwark. Her uncle now lives there and Henry's approached him about the possibility that you may take up residence there. Mr Scott, the younger, has agreed." She sees the uncertain look on my face. "You will be away from the horrors that will shortly stalk the city but you'll still be close enough to visit Robert if ….. if ……"

She means, if Robert survives the executions but her voice fades away as she cannot contemplate the deaths of any, or possibly all, of the remaining members of her family.

A week later we go down to the wharf to take the wherry across the Thames on the first stage of our short journey to Camberwell. Our small items of baggage have gone ahead over London Bridge.

"I do not know why we couldn't have ridden over the bridge to Camberwell," says Amy, as the oarsmen push the boat from the jetty.

As if in answer there's a most horrible screaming from somewhere in the city and, looking up, we see an assortment of body parts and heads on pikes displayed on London Bridge. Queen Mary's reprisals have only just begun.

Chapter Twelve
Camberwell

When we arrive at the house of the Scott family we're pleasantly surprised. Though built in the old style it's surrounded by pretty gardens and orchards and the family is as friendly as Amy's cousins in the city were cold and unwelcoming. Mrs Picto and James are already here with the horses and mules and our two trunks of clothing. The animals have been stabled in a mews over the coldest winter months and Amy is delighted to see her little mare, Pavane, again. She fondles the horse's grey mane and rubs her shoulders affectionately and Pavane makes the little snickering sound that horses reserve for the people they like.

"She was given to me by Robert just before our wedding," Amy explains to her cousins and uncle, "And she's always looked after me. She has perfect manners and is so gentle. Robert trained her himself."

"How old is she, Lady Amy?" says Thomas, the youngest boy.

"Just five years old."

"Can I ride her too?"

"Only if you're very gentle!" says Amy, pretending to be very stern. And everyone laughs as Thomas claps his hands with excitement at the anticipated thrill.

Pavane is taken away by James and stabled with my horse, my solid reliable Bess, and the mules. We know that we'll be happy in this warm hearted family as they show us proudly round their house and tell amusing tales of Amy's grandfather who must have been quite a lively but kindly old gentleman.

Unfortunately, in the coming days, we find that we're not completely isolated from the events in the city for, walking in the garden on the cold and sunny days of early March, we can still hear the blood curdling screams of tortured, dying men on the other side of the river. We take to spending long periods indoors.

The news is dire. All the rebellious Whitecoats have been hanged at the doors of their own houses. Other rebels are being butchered on a daily basis, their limbs displayed in every conceivable public place, Charing Cross, the gates to the city, all the crossroads and London Bridge. Even less fortunate are the men hanged in chains and left to die. Crows and rats are having a feast and the warmer weather of the approaching spring promises swarms of flies and the spread of disease. London will be the most unpleasant place to live in all England.

Henry Sidney comes to visit us with some important news that's not entirely to Amy's liking. Lady Elizabeth has been arrested on suspicion of participation in the Wyatt plot. At first Amy smiles and nods, "I thought as much. She's totally untrustworthy. At last someone has seen through her."

Henry gives her a sharp look and then imparts a piece of news that Amy finds most unwelcome. Elizabeth is being held in the Tower not far from Robert's lodgings.

"Surely she's not allowed to talk to the brothers?" asks Amy in a panic and Henry reassures her that Elizabeth is in fear of her life and suffering from ill health so she is most certainly not interested in social intercourse.

The good news is that Amy may once again visit Robert and that Henry Sidney is working with Prince Philip to secure the release of all of the brothers now that it has been established that they were not involved in the plot in any way.

And so it is that we find ourselves crossing the Thames on a cold April morning to disembark at the Tower wharf. Amy has not seen Robert since before Christmas so it's a touching scene as they embrace and hold each other tightly as if they will never allow anyone to part them ever again. The Lieutenant Warden asks us if we would like to join him for dinner while Amy and Robert talk in private.

"So what news does Robert have?" I ask on the journey back across the Thames, as we wave farewell to Henry on the wharf. I'm careful not to mention Elizabeth's name.

"He says the Tower's been so crowded with prisoners for the past few weeks that the smell was unbearable but now so many of them have been tried and executed that it's getting back to normal. He says that he and his brothers are allowed to walk out again and the first thing he did was to walk down to the menagerie to see the porkie-pines."

"The what?"

"Porkie-pines. He says they're like giant hedgehogs and they like apples. He bought apples for them in the autumn but now there's nothing for them until the harvest in September."

"How strange. God made some very peculiar animals."

"None as strange as mankind."

111

There's a pause and then Amy says, "He saw Elizabeth when she was brought into the Tower. He says she looked terrified and angry at the same time and she looked at the scaffold where Jane was executed as she walked past. He was very sorry to see her so."

"Is she allowed the freedom to walk outside?"

"No, well not yet. She has very comfortable lodgings but they've put her in the apartments her mother used before she was executed."

"How cruel."

"Yes. Her life is in the balance. Each day she's questioned about her part in the plot but even Wyatt himself has refused to implicate her and claims she's innocent and knew nothing."

"What do you think?"

"It's hard to say. After all, Wyatt intended to depose Mary and put Elizabeth on the throne. She probably knew something but Robert believes that Mary will think again before executing her. Elizabeth still has many allies and a huge following among the evangelicals so there could be another uprising if her life is threatened. Anyway enough about Elizabeth! She's no longer important because – you will not believe this, Kate! – when Robert is released from the Tower, we are going to live in Norfolk. We'll have our own manor house in the countryside close to my family and away from all the plotting of the court."

I can't believe my ears when I hear this. Robert was tried for treason after his brothers but found guilty and attainted nevertheless. As a result of this attainder Robert now has no fortune of his own and no property anywhere. In effect, he and Amy are penniless and we're all dependent on the charity of their relatives in order to live. Where will they obtain the money to buy a manor house?

Amy reads my mind and says, "Robert says that he would make a pact with the devil in order to revive our fortunes. Oh don't look like that, Kate. He's merely jesting. He means that soon Queen Mary will marry her Spanish prince and he will be Prince Philip's loyal servant until we're restored in blood to the Dudley lands and titles."

I nod sagely as if I understand all but, deep down, it makes no sense. First there is the small matter of religion. Robert is from an evangelical family while Mary and Philip are committed Catholics so why would they wish to have Robert to work for them? What makes Robert think that he and his brothers will have a role to play?

Unless ….. unless – I can hardly believe this but I've heard it said – Philip intends to draw England into his ambitions in Europe and use our young men to fight his wars for him. What's gone on between Henry Sidney, the Spaniards and the Dudley brothers? And does the Queen know of Philip's plans? Indeed, is this the reason why Prince Philip, a young man, is marrying her, a woman most people would admit is now too old to have children. Is this the real reason for the marriage?

And Robert himself, can he be deceiving Amy into believing that he'll soon settle down? To me it sounds as if he's even more calculating than he ever was and the life of a Lord of the Manor in Norfolk will never suit his soaring ambitions - even if he survives the Tower.

My thoughts are interrupted by Amy's cheerful voice. "Robert says that when he's released he'll

113

have revenge on those people who turned traitor to his father, Arundel and Pembroke and the like. He's carving a motto on the wall of his prison. 'O Mightie Lord to whom all vengeance doth belong.' Oh look there's Harry Scott waiting for us by the wharf."

She waves wildly to her kinsman. That's Amy, madly optimistic or in the depths of despair, but never in between!

Chapter Thirteen
Freedom and Poverty

Wyatt's been executed and his boiled head placed on a spike on London Bridge, only for it to be stolen the following day. The executions continue but the Queen's decided to be merciful and pardons some of the poorer rebels from Kent when they parade before her with ropes round their necks to beg for mercy.

The city of London has been a grisly sight with body parts festooned in every public place and the smell is stomach turning. Even seasoned soldiers are revolted and our family avoids the city at all costs. But by spring Queen Mary has other things to think about as she prepares for her forthcoming marriage to Prince Philip; she orders the gibbets to be taken down and the cleaning up to begin. Elizabeth's been spared the executioner's axe due to lack of evidence and is banished to house arrest far away from court at Woodstock near Oxford. Ironically it's Mary's change in the law that saves Elizabeth's life; from now on, the Queen has decreed, no one will be convicted of treason on an accusation unless full proof can be found. Elizabeth's been lucky again but the Queen is not fooled.

Queen Mary marries her prince in July 1554 at Winchester Cathedral far away from any London protesters. She now believes that all evangelicals are trouble causers, says Henry Sidney, on one of our visits to his London residence, and he's having a difficult time at court concealing his beliefs. Strangely enough it's Philip and the Spanish courtiers who are his friends and protectors. They've promised to do all they can to secure the release of the remaining Dudley brothers from the Tower.

There's some other good news too. Mary Sidney is expecting the birth of her first child and Henry says, if the baby is a boy, he will name him Philip to show his gratitude to the family's benefactor.

The summer passes slowly and uneventfully. Amy continues to visit Robert and enjoys a new peace of mind now that Elizabeth is far away. By the end of the summer there's more joyful news; the Queen is apparently already pregnant and in her happiness, she's been persuaded by Philip to release Robert and his brothers.

The Scott's home becomes a flurry of activity as Amy's little household prepares for the move to Penshurst Place where Mary Sidney and Lady Dudley, the former Duchess of Northumberland, are now residing. Henry's going to bring his brothers-in-law to the family home in Kent where we'll all be reunited and Amy can scarcely conceal her excitement.

"It'll be wonderful for all our kin to be together again," says Amy. "You know, Kate, I think that I won't even mind his mother's sharp tongue from now on!"

But there's a tragedy looming. When Henry and the Dudley brothers arrive at Penshurst we have no real cause for celebration; first Ambrose has not yet been released and then we find that John, the oldest, has a fever caught from the bad air in the Tower and is very ill. His freedom turns out to be short lived and he dies a few weeks after his release. Lady Dudley's hysterical in her grief. An air of gloom descends over Penshurst Place.

116

There's further bad news for Amy as she hears that her beloved father has also died. Her half brother John Appleyard together with Sir John Robsart's illegitimate son, Arthur Robsart, arrive in Kent to break the bad news to their sister and Amy is devastated with grief and guilt; she's not seen her father since before Robert's imprisonment, always intending to visit him when we were staying at Mr Hyde's house in Throcking. "Poor father. Poor father," sobs Amy, "I should have been with him when he died."

John Appleyard explains to her, gently, that Sir John died suddenly and there was nothing anyone could do. His own mother, Lady Elizabeth, who's also Amy's mother, will inherit Syderstone and the vast Robsart estate in Norfolk to which Amy is the sole heir when her mother dies. I feel sorry for Arthur who's now dependent on the charity of his deceased father's family and can expect nothing for himself. This was, of course, Northumberland's doing when the marriage settlement was thrashed out before Robert and Amy married. Poor Arthur stands by quietly while John explains the situation to Amy; he is fond of, but hardly close to, his natural sister.

On the other hand all the Appleyard children saw Amy as the baby of the family after their mother was remarried to John Robsart - and spoiled her considerably when she was small! The Appleyard house, Stanfield Hall, will become theirs and not Amy's when their mother dies so there's no rivalry between them and their half sister.

Christmas 1554 arrives and despite the birth of Mary Sidney's child, a son named Philip, we're all subdued for the second year running. Ambrose, tired and ill, is released from prison and joins his brothers just before Christmas and together they mourn the death of John. Robert and Ambrose are delighted with the new baby since they have no children of their own and there's a wistful sadness as Ambrose remembers the deaths of his own baby daughter and then his first wife. Elizabeth Tailboys, his second wife, is a wealthy baroness in her own right and has been allowed by the Queen to retain her land and property in Lincolnshire, despite being married to a Dudley. But personal happiness in the form of a family has not yet been granted to the couple as, indeed, it has not to Amy and Robert.

We all adore young Philip and make plans for his future. His mother is a talented writer and poet so will the baby inherit his mother's intellect, we wonder? Robert seems mesmerised by the little one and spends time holding his tiny hand and talking to him as if he can understand, much to everyone's amusement. Lady Dudley, however, has become very frail and weak and is too ill to pay the new arrival any attention; she is still consumed with grief over the death of John but manages the strength to write to Prince Philip to thank him for delivering her sons from the Tower and to ask him to protect them in the event of her death. The result is that Ambrose and Robert are summoned to court again to take part in the festivities celebrating the twelve nights of Christmas, which may go on well into January! Amy is once more downcast at the prospect of another separation from Robert.

Prince Philip has planned an exhibition of jousting and fighting with canes, popular among the Spanish nobles at court, and intends to entertain the

English courtiers over the Christmas holiday. This will be an opportunity to show off the athleticism and fighting skills of Philip's own men but they have to have opponets to fight against. The two brothers are more than eager to take part, in the hope that they will restore the Dudley family fortunes by befriending the Spaniards. To Amy's dismay they set out for London immediately.

By the end of January they're back at Penshurst for their mother's funeral and Robert and Amy have a shock in store. Lady Dudley's will practically ignores them and all they can expect is a very small amount each year to live on. Everyone else in the family has been provided for and has been left some small token of their mother's affection despite the fact that Lady Dudley had little to spare after her husband's execution and had accumulated several debts.

"It's because Robert did not arrest Princess Mary when his father sent him into Norfolk," wails Amy.

"But he couldn't be blamed for that. Northumberland was too slow and Mary guessed his plan. She fled several days before he even realised she'd gone. And Robert was just twenty one. John and Ambrose were older and more suited to the task. The Duke should have sent his older sons."

"He thought Robert was dispensible," says Amy bitterly, "Because of his marriage to me, Kat. He didn't have the fine prospects of the other sons. Even Henry the youngest had married a rich heiress. I don't think Lady Dudley liked me much. Now what will we do?"

Well I really have no idea. We can't live on the charity of other people forever.

119

While we're pondering our own problems, there's bad news from court. In an attempt to show the strength of her Catholic faith and dissuade any further Protestant rebellions, Mary has persuaded her Council, now a huge body of forty or so committed Catholics bent on imposing religious discipline, to sanction the burnings of heretics – that is to say, us. The first is a preacher from St Paul's, John Rogers, who's burned on the 4th February 1555 at Smithfield and we're horrified to learn that the poor man died with his wife and children looking on and calling encouragement to him in his torment. We learn even more dreadful details later; how the wind blew the flames away from him and the poor man had been slowly burned alive, only dying after almost an hour of the most horrific agony. Then there are more burnings; Bishop Hooper in Gloucester as well as other Protestant clergy in Coventry and Suffolk. We're shocked that the Queen, who showed mercy to rebels and indeed to our own family, can be so cruel to her fellow loyal countrymen merely for following their own religious beliefs.

In April there are more burnings in Chester and, in May, still more in Smithfield. Queen Mary's bloody ridding of religious offenders is spreading all over the country and it seems that no one will be safe. Ordinary tradesmen and apprentices are the latest victims. Butchers, barbers, weavers are all asked to renounce their beliefs and all refuse. This isn't what Mary had in mind; she wanted to demonstrate how weak we Protestants are in our faith; instead of which all the condemned men are prepared to face a hideous death rather than recant. Amy's ashamed that

Robert's father betrayed his faith to try to save his neck.

The burnings have the opposite effect to the fearful subservience Mary had intended. They inspire rebellion. One gentleman named Thomas Haukes was asked to lift his hand above his head if the pain of the fire was tolerable. As the flames engulfed him he raised both hands and clapped them together in a gesture of triumph. The onlookers cheered and clapped with him.

Closer to home we have no desire to make martyrs of ourselves. Mary Sidney says that Henry's warned her to follow the old style of religious ceremony in our chapel, restoring candles, pictures, images and the Latin mass. This is, says Henry, no time for heroism. The walls have ears and servants and friends are being encouraged to report any acts of 'heresy' to the authorities.

After the Christmas festivities at court and Lady Dudley's funeral Ambrose and Elizabeth Tailboys returned to her property in Lincolnshire while Robert and Amy decided to stay here at Penshurst Place, having nowhere else to go. Young Henry Dudley has moved to his wife's relatives in Essex. Henry Sidney was hoping that the Queen's coming confinement for the birth of her child would cause her to relent in her persecution of Protestant clergy but, as the time approaches, the burnings increase.

On 30th April there's a welcome sound as church bells ring out and word is spread that the Queen has been delivered of a baby boy. "Thank Jesus," says Mary Sidney, "Now perhaps she will be restored to her right mind and the persecution will stop." We order a great feast for the servants and hear that, in

London, there are feastings and celebrations in the streets.

But there's no sign of the new baby. The Queen and Prince have not been seen in public and gradually there's a general realisation that there is no heir to the throne, merely a false rumour spread from who knows where.

As spring changes to summer, Queen Mary announces that she's been mistaken in her dates and that the baby will now be born later than she'd thought.

By mid-summer her nerves are obviously frayed. There's still no sign of the birth. Even worse Robert, Ambrose and Henry, who'd been meeting some of their friends and supporters in the St Paul's area of the city, have been ordered to leave London and not to set foot in it again on pain of death. Queen Mary obviously suspects that Robert, as a Dudley and by all accounts a drunken, brawling Dudley at that, is too great a focus for rebellion to be trusted. That's just the news we didn't need.

"You were doing so well. Getting along with Philip and the other Spaniards; and the Spanish ambassador, Feria, who's done so much for us. What were you thinking of? What were you doing at St Paul's anyway?" reproves Amy when Robert returns to Penshurst.

"Kindly refrain from speaking to me like that, Amy. Remember that I'm your husband and what I do in the city is my own business. And I'll meet whoever I chose - without your approval." With this Robert stamps out.

"He's meeting rebellious factions, I know," says Amy with a worried frown. "I know he is, Kate.

He's just like his father, always plotting and gambling on the future. It's like a giant game of cards to him but with higher stakes."

That evening Henry Sidney calls us all together to talk about the future. He has to stay in favour with the Queen and therefore must distance himself from any suggestion of dissent. He'll follow the official policy as far as religion and support for Prince Philip is concerned. There's a snort of disapproval when he says this and it's from Robert.

"I will never, never compromise my beliefs for anyone," he says scornfully. "Yes I like Philip and Feria but I won't become a supporter of anyone who favours a return to Rome and idolatry."

"That's not what the Spanish want us to do. They're more practical than that. They merely want to have the English as allies against France," says Henry. "What's more they're advising Mary to desist from this policy of burning so-called heretics. They know it will not succeed in subduing people and will lead to rebellion. Even Prince Philip's confessor has publicly condemned the burnings but Mary and Bishop Gardiner take no notice. In London and Essex there's been yet another spate of executions."

"Queen Mary doesn't think the same as her husband," says Robert. "She's determined to crush anyone who opposes her restoration of the Pope as head of our church in England. She won't stop with burning bishops, preachers and the poor and weak, Henry. Just listen to what I say. It'll be the rest of us next. The recent martyrs for our Protestant cause were no willing martyrs at all, simply defenceless people reported by their neighbours and even their kin for still following the evangelical form of worship.

We'll all be at the mercy of servants, common people, money-lenders, anyone who bears us a grudge in fact. And I, for one, do not intend to wait around for someone to report me to the magistrates or her spies on the Privy Council."

"She'll soften when the baby's born," says Henry confidently, "You'll see. We'll have an heir for England and all will be peaceful again."

Robert gives a snort of derision. "An heir? A baby? There are many who believe this baby is just wind and that there's no baby after all. Even if there were, what would it mean? A Catholic Prince brought up to be as peevish as his mother. I'd rather not witness that!"

"Be quiet Robert. You're too hot headed in these matters. If you feel so strongly you must find lodgings elsewhere, with your brothers or your friends. I won't have my family brought into any plots regarding the Queen."

"Oh Henry, no! Please allow Robert to stay here with us. He's my brother and mother left him with so little to live on. How will he and Amy get by?" says Mary desperately.

"Pray don't trouble yourselves in my direction. We'll manage as we always do." Robert is proud, angry and on his dignity. "Very well; we wouldn't put your household at risk, Henry. Amy, take Katherine and Mrs Picto with you and pack the chests. We'll return to your cousins in Camberwell. We don't wish to stay where we're not wanted."

So it is that we end up once more at the Scotts, and then with Henry and Margaret Audley for a while, and then to the Hydes at Throcking, and then to the house of Ambrose and Elizabeth in

124

Lincolnshire and finally to Stanfield Hall, the home of Amy's mother, where we hear in November 1555 that Ambrose has, with the approval of Henry and Robert's uncle, Sir Andrew Dudley, given the manor of Hales Owen, his inheritance from his mother, to Robert. Queen Mary in a characteristic act of unexpected generosity had allowed Lady Dudley to keep possession of Hales Owen despite her husband's treason.

Such an act of kindness on behalf of Ambrose was totally unexpected. Robert and Amy are overwhelmed and relieved. Our precarious financial position is alleviated by the revenue from the Hales Owen manor and its farm lands and we will never again be poor and dependent on the charity of others.

Chapter Fourteen
Separation – Spring 1556

Christmas 1555 is a time of great happiness for Amy and Robert. They have decided to look for a manor house of their own in Norfolk and Robert's now able to buy for Amy the kind of clothes that she once wore when his father was the most influential man in the land. One of her presents is a beautiful diamond pendant and there are pretty gloves and a new saddle of leather and velvet for her horse. I haven't seen Amy so animated for a long time.

Robert also has a career to look forward to. He's acting as a courier for Prince Philip who had departed for the Low Countries several months earlier, soon after it became clear that his wife's pregnancy had been a figment of her imagination. Queen Mary is beside herself with grief and it's obvious to all at court that her love for Philip is greater, much greater, than his love for the Queen. Robert's new role involves him in a lot of travelling to and from the continent to do the Prince's bidding but Amy's happy because her husband is happy; she hopes to see him from time to time when he delivers letters to ambassadors and other influential people at court.

The news from court is dreadful, however. The old bishops, Latimer and Ridley, have been burned outside the walls of Oxford and, in March 1556, Archbishop Cranmer follows them to the bonfire. The old man, having been forced to watch the agonising death of his friends, had fearfully recanted many times, denouncing his Protestant faith and hoping that his life would be spared. The Queen was triumphant knowing that this would send a strong message to other rebels and Protestants. However, Cranmer heard that his recantation would not mitigate his punishment and, in a brave speech before his execution, he had addressed the congregation and once more denounced the evils of Catholicism as he saw them. At his execution he held his right hand into the flames so that it would suffer first for signing the documents of recantation. It was a powerful image of defiance and not one that Queen Mary wanted.

And Robert was quite correct. Mary has now burned more and more ordinary people all over England, many reported for their religious lapses by jealous neighbours and one time friends. The fires of Smithfield in London are causing much suffering and we're glad to be far away from all the horror.

The Queen had so wanted a royal heir but her confinement never took place and there had been no baby, the whole disaster inspired by her desire to please her husband and her unwillingness to accept that her swollen stomach might be the result of illness or disease. In early August the court had moved from Hampton Court where the birth of the baby had been much anticipated all summer long. All the women hired to help with the new baby were dismissed and the crib sent away. Elizabeth, who'd been ordered to travel to court to support her sister during her confinement, now returned home to Hatfield.

There'd been no celebrations at court during Christmas 1555. Philip's return to the Spanish held Low Countries had caused the Queen to be, so they said, heartbroken at the double loss of husband and much longed-for child. There had been no masques, dancing and jousting this year. The Queen is now miserable and completely depressed.

Amy, though initially pleased for Robert, is destined soon to share the Queen's sense of abandonment. After Christmas we moved back to Mr Hyde's house at Throcking and Robert began to spend long periods away from home with his brothers or with his uncle – or so he says. Amy's too afraid to ask what his business is and allows him to go, unquestioned.

By March a comet has been seen blazing across the sky, warning us of civil strife and unrest, and we hear that parts of London have been set alight by a gang of malcontents. Even here in the pleasant countryside of Hertfordshire, people are predicting another accursed summer like the last, with rain and floods spoiling the harvest and causing famine. There are mutterings that this is God's vengeance on a state that condemns ordinary Christian folk to be burned alive and the comet is just a warning of worse things to come. News of Cranmer's death has spread and the Queen is becoming a figure of hatred.

Finally another crisis erupts for our family with the news of another anti-government plot. Amy's only too aware that Robert, on his infrequent visits home, has spent much of the time in the company of his men, playing cards and talking late into the night or making strange and unaccountable journeys out and about the Hertfordshire countryside. Even worse, we hear that Elizabeth, who is still at Hatfield House, has been implicated in the conspiracy as has Robert's cousin, Sir Henry Dudley. Hatfield is a mere ten miles from Throcking!

Of the Dudley brothers there's now no sign but a warrant is out for their arrest and their cousin Henry, who's fled to the continent, has been declared a traitor.

Amy's distracted as the weeks progress and still there's no word of Robert or his brothers. She had become accustomed to his prolonged absences but this new development is simply a repetition of the past – the possibility of the Dudley kin involved in rebellion against the monarch. By May we hear that Elizabeth's gentlewomen have been arrested and that the princess is once more under house arrest on suspicion of treason. Kat Ashley, Elizabeth's closest friend, has been found to be concealing large amounts of seditious literature in her apartments at Somerset House, all calling for rebellion against the rumoured coronation of Prince Philip and against the restoration of Popish rule in England. Elizabeth's fate seems to be sealed.

"But where is Robert? Where is he? Where is he?" moans Amy pacing the Long Gallery at Throcking, "Is he to remain a fugitive all his life and what am I to do? Oh I knew that Elizabeth would be his undoing. I warned him. I warned him. Oh she is an evil woman, Kat. She's evil. I know now what he's been involved in, why he wanted us to be close to her house at Hatfield. What a fool he's been. And what will we do? He's sure to be arrested and executed for this. Oh I can't bear it, Kat. What ever will I do?"

In May a message arrives by an anonymous source to say that Robert is safe and well in Flanders. But what really surprises us is the news from court that Elizabeth's been forgiven for her part in the conspiracy, which was obvious to all even though she made feverish denials of her involvement, and that her sister, Mary, has sent her a large diamond to show that she believes her explanation of ignorance and innocence!

"Why would the Queen believe her, Kat? She cannot be so stupid. Why is Elizabeth so suddenly forgiven? She's been causing trouble for years. I would have thought that Mary would have been glad of an excuse to get rid of her. *I* for one would be more than happy to see her head roll off the block."

"No, no. Just think for a moment, Amy. Prince Philip – I suppose I should say King Philip of Spain now since his father's retirement – has obviously intervened on Elizabeth's behalf and Mary can deny him nothing."

"Why would he do that? What's Elizabeth to Philip?"

"She's nothing other than his protection against the French. Mary's getting older and, by all accounts, is not well at all. If she dies and Elizabeth is executed, their young cousin Mary Stuart, Queen of the Scots, is next in the succession to the throne of England. With a French mother and already betrothed to the Dauphin, she'll be allied to the French who are Philip's enemies. Of course Philip does not wish to see a huge English-French-Scottish state to rival Spain and the Holy Roman Emperor. Of course he doesn't want Elizabeth dead."

"Well that's not what I want," wails Amy.

So we'll just have to see if the Queen, in time, will forgive the Dudley brothers too and whether Philip will still show them favour when, or rather *if,* he returns to England from the Low Countries. Mary

Sidney writes to us with the news from London. There've been more Protestant burnings at Smithfield and some hideous atrocities on the island of Guernsey where it's reported that a new born baby was cast into the flames with his mother and her kin.

Queen Mary, says Amy's sister-in-law, now looks old beyond her years with loneliness and worry. She's haggard and thin and cannot sleep. Although some of the ring leaders of the conspiracy have been rounded up and executed, there are others at large. She does not mention any names so we still have no idea of the extent to which Robert and his brothers were involved with their cousin, Henry Dudley's, plot nor have we any idea where they are now. The queen hides herself away and begs her husband to return to England but Philip is now after a bigger prize. He has already been crowned King of Spain by his father and now wishes Mary to crown him King of England too. Mary knows that this would be disastrous for her reign and is reconciled to a life alone.

"Well I know how she feels," says Amy downheartedly as we pack our belongings once again for a summer visit to her sister Anne's household.

Chapter Fifteen
1557 - A New Year

By Christmas 1556, there's still no sign of Robert but
we do have news of his whereabouts. Apparently
he's been working with Prince Philip's courtiers in
the Low Countries and has been seen with the Earl of
Pembroke in the English-held port of Calais, France,
inspecting the fortifications on behalf of the Queen's
Council. Amy is considerably relieved.

We're now with Amy's mother at Stanfield Hall
in Norfolk. The daily Christmas celebrations are
enjoyable with players performing masques to music,
dancing, a story teller who recounts the tale of Sir
Gawain and the green knight (Amy squeals with
horror as the green knight's head, a turnip painted and
decorated with animal fur, rolls down the Great Hall!)
and a company of village mummers who perform a
play that's simply mimed to music and a strange
mixture of comedy and folk story.

Amy loves these entertainments and claps with
delight when the doctor restores to life the Turk slain
by St George. The doctor pours a potion from a small
bottle down the throat of the Turk and indicates to us
all that it will revive the dead man. And indeed it
does, for the Turk gets up and fights again! Amy's
animated and flushed with the fun of the evening and,
still not knowing who the mummers truly are, we all
sit down with them for a feast of a supper in the Great
Hall. The leftovers are collected and given to the
company to take home.

Apart from the lack of contact from Robert and
the absence of gifts from Robert to Amy, the festive
season passes pleasantly. Amy's now resigned to

Robert's permanent absence and the news from court predicts that the Queen will soon have other matters to occupy her as King Philip of Spain picks a quarrel with the Pope by allowing the Duke of Alva to invade the Papal States. Pope Paul IV asks for French help and Douai in the Low Countries, held by the Spanish, is attacked by the French. It is an act of war, a war that England will have to fight with Philip against France and he loses no time requesting the necessary assistance from his wife, Queen Mary.

By March 1557, however, there's much better news. Robert has been sent to the Queen by Philip to deliver the joyful news that the Prince has decided to return to England within the next few days. Queen Mary's overjoyed and, as the bearer of good tidings, Robert is completely in her favour at last. Amy and I are now back at the Hyde household in Throcking while Robert lives at Christchurch, a house in London owned by his brother Henry's wife, Margaret Audley. It's conveniently close to court and Robert's Spanish masters. But Prince Philip is now expecting repayment from the Dudley brothers for the friendship he's shown them in the past and is about to call in the debt.

Amy, however, is preoccupied with other matters. Her mother's just died meaning that Amy can now claim her inheritance from her father, all the vast lands in Norfolk and the tumbledown manor house at Syderstone. It's enough to ensure a visit northwards by Robert who will, of course, be the true inheritor of his wife's property. And, by the end of May, Robert's been on a spending spree! Not only has he sold off part of Amy's vast estate but he's borrowed from money lenders, mortgaged parts of the

Hales Owen estate and, in July, he mortgages the whole of the Hales Owen manor to a friend of his, called Mr Forster who has a reputation for honesty and straight dealing.

"Robert, now that we have so much money, may we begin to look for a manor of our own," pleads Amy.

"Of course we can, my love. Just be patient and everything will work out for us," replies her husband.

A man called Thomas Blount who looks after Robert's financial matters, as he had done for Robert's father many years before, comes to visit us at Throcking and the two men sit up late into the night talking. The following day, while the gentlemen of the house are out hunting, Amy opens Robert's account books and glances through them. There are many payments she can't understand and what's more these are very large amounts. She's furious.

When she's alone with Robert that evening and Blount's returned to London with the accounts, she confronts her husband about the payments and there's another violent argument with Robert claiming that this is none of her business and Amy declaring that, since part of the money has come from her father's estate, it *is* her business. Amy's suspicions over Elizabeth are once again on the surface as she remembers Robert's recent business trips around Throcking Manor where gossip is rife concerning the Lady Elizabeth and the way she's being kept a virtual prisoner at Hatfield with a few loyal friends, a small number of paid servants and little personal money to hire more. Elizabeth has many properties but no ready cash and Amy suspects that Robert's using her inheritance to subsidise his former friend.

The argument becomes more and more heated until Robert says, "I'll tell you what the money's for, my lady. You sit at home enjoying an idle life ordering gloves and ribbons as you please while I'm left to ensure the safety of our family and, as such, I've had to promise allegiance to Prince Philip in the forthcoming war with France and these matters cost money. An army doesn't pay for itself."

"War with France! Army? What are you talking about, Robert? We're not at war with France. The Council would never agree to it," says Amy.

"Apparently, they did, especially when Queen Mary threatened the Privy Counsellors with treason if they refused."

"She can deny Prince Philip nothing," says Amy.

"Yes she's a good wife in that respect," says Robert bitterly. Amy is stung by this and says nothing.

"Anyway," continues Robert, "You needn't concern yourself on my behalf. Blount tells me that war was declared five days ago so tomorrow I travel back to London where I'll meet up with my bothers, Ambrose and Henry. We're to serve under the Earl of Pembroke on the frontier in Flanders. You may soon be rid of me for ever."

"Oh no, Robert! Please don't leave like this just when we have all we need to make us happy. Please don't go just yet. Please. Just one more day so we can make up these differences ….."

But Amy's wasting her breath. A door bangs shut as Robert goes into the chamber vacated by Thomas Blount. There's the sound of a key turning in the lock. When Amy shows her swollen, tear-stained face at breakfast, Robert's already on the road, riding hard for London.

Chapter Sixteen
A Family Tragedy

Amy's been in a dreadful state since Robert's departure and is consumed by guilt at the way in which they parted. She's heard that there has been fierce fighting in Flanders and has no idea whether any or all the Dudley brothers are safe. However she has to pull herself together as there's now no one to manage her father's estate at Syderstone. Ironically she now has it all to herself and, upon being reminded that Robert had debts to be settled, she writes a business letter to Mr Flowerdew, the estate manager. Amy, at twenty five, has now grown up.

"Mr Flowerdew,

I understand from Gryse that you told him to remind me about the matter of the sale of sheep from Syderstone which I forgot to ask my lord about before he left as he was troubled with weighty affairs and I was in a desperate state at his sudden departure. I have now to take that decision myself and trust you as a friend when you say that we should sell the wool as soon as possible. Do so immediately even if it means selling at a lower price than we would normally expect. My lord required me before leaving to pay these poor men everything he owes them and to do so urgently so I do not mind sustaining a loss to fulfil his wishes. My lord wanted the money to be sent to Gryse in London. I'm sorry to be always troubling you and, until such time as I may repay you, I send you my thanks. So to God I leave you,

From Mr Hyde's, 7th August
Amy Dudley"

Amy is determined now to do all she can to please Lord Robert. She has no idea where this money is going but knows that it is needed to settle an urgent debt. Her jealousy of Elizabeth is forgotten for now and she prays every day for her husband's safe return.

Still there's no news.

Summer passes into autumn but we won't be helping with the harvest as we once did. The girlish Amy who once took such a delight in apple picking and preserve making is beginning to look tired and drawn with worry. She has little interest in life and looks much older than her years. The illness that affects her when she's distressed, returns and her breasts swell and are painful.

"Are you sure, Amy, that you are not with child?" asks Mrs Hyde.

Amy shakes her head sadly and returns to her chamber, away from the curious stares of the women in the household.

In September we hear that the Earl of Pembroke and his men are to join forces with the Spaniards near St Quentin on the Flemish border but we do not know if Robert is still with this army. The town is being held by the French and Philip's soldiers face a huge battle and a siege to take it back.

October comes and, at last, there's news but it's very bad news. Mary Sidney sends a messenger to tell us that her youngest brother, Henry, the darling of the family, has been killed outside St Quentin. She believes that Ambrose and Robert are still alive but has no more information other than what some of the early returning troops have said – that it was the worst fighting they had ever seen.

"Oh poor Henry and poor Margaret. They're both so young," says Amy.

"I'll always remember the fear on Henry's face when we saw them riding down the road from Cambridge after he was arrested with his father and brothers. He was only sixteen then. I wonder if Robert knows about his death– he'll be distraught."

My question is answered when, two weeks later, Robert returns to Mr. Hyde's house. But he's not the Robert who left at the end of June. Haggard and thin, moody and silent, greeting only Mr Hyde with the briefest of courtesies, Robert slumps at the large oak table and shovels spoons of the cook's rabbit broth into his mouth in a most uncouth manner, as if he is digging in the garden and disposing of each spade load down his throat.

Uncertainly Amy walks over to him and places her hand on his shoulder but he looks at it and then at her as if he doesn't know who she is. Amy takes her hand away and, giving me a worried look, stands a little way off, observing him. As soon as Robert's finished his broth, he stands, picks up his cloak and, without a word, strides off up the stairs where we hear the door of his chamber close and the bolt drawn.

Mr Hyde looks at Amy sympathetically and takes her hand.

"Try not to trouble yourself too much about this, Amy. I've known it before when men come home after a bloody battle. They're in shock and it affects their brain for a while – a temporary madness – but it will pass. Try not to approach him when he doesn't wish for company and just leave him to his own thoughts for a while. We will all have to bear with him."

So for three weeks Robert comes down for his meals, occasionally walks around the garden a couple of times, and then returns to his own chamber. The servants leave the hall silently when he appears; they're frightened of him and he looks so wild and dishevelled that Amy and I are not surprised. Occasionally Amy, who waits upon him at the table, will ask, "Robert my love, would you like this bread?" …… or this jelly, or an apple, or some more broth or whatever. The response is always the same. He looks at her as if he'd forgotten she was there, can't understand which language she is talking and is wondering where he's seen her before. It's frightening.

Towards the middle of November there's a day which is unusually sunny and warm for the time of year. Amy and I decide to spend some time in the garden and take a bag to pick some of the herbs before the frost kills them off. We plan to dry them in the bread oven as it cools down and preserve them for the winter months. Rounding a corner we encounter Robert sitting on a bench, hunched forward, his head in his hands. From the way his shoulders are shaking it's obvious he's crying.

We try to back away quietly up the path before he sees us. We know that fighting men resent anyone seeing them in this state and Robert has always had the reputation for being the most fearless and athletic in the lists and in the tournaments fought at court. But he lifts his head and his sad and tearful eyes are looking straight at us. Without a word he stretches out his arm and holds out his hand for Amy to take.

Before I can embarrass him with my presence I turn and walk away.

The following day Amy tells me that they are travelling to see Henry Dudley's widow, Margaret Audley, at her home Christchurch in London. Queen Mary was, by all accounts, shocked to hear of young Henry's death and, in gratitude for the loyalty that the family's shown to Prince Philip, has forgiven the two remaining Dudley brothers, Ambrose and Robert. This means that the attainder which was placed on the whole family after the Lady Jane Grey affair has now been lifted and they can all have back the family property that was confiscated. Once again the Queen has shown herself to be a strange mixture of compassion to her one time enemies and vindictiveness to heretics who are still being burned in even larger numbers.

"Once we have inherited our property," says Amy, "We will be free to choose a manor of our own in Norfolk. Just imagine it, Kat! A beautiful house of our own, fruit trees, a little garden and a deer park - plenty of hunting land for Robert."

"Has Robert agreed to this?" I'm astonished.

"Yes – he says he'll no longer have to fight wars for others to make a living and never wants to see another battlefield. Henry's widow has offered him the use of Christchurch in London because she can't bear to be there – it has too many memories of Henry. So Robert can have it and he'll sometimes go there when he wants to be alone to resume his studies of mathematics or we'll both go there when we need to be at court. But most of the time we'll live as Lord and Lady of the manor here in Norfolk."

I could never have imagined Robert Dudley settling down as Lord of the Manor in some sleepy part of Norfolk but I expect that the war has made him see life in a different light. After all, Amy tells me, at St Quentin he saw Henry blown to pieces by a cannonball while the two of them stood side by side.

Chapter Seventeen
January 1558

Amy and Robert returned to Throcking before Christmas 1557 and now intend to start their search for a manor in the spring. For perhaps the first time since their marriage almost eight years ago they seem happy and contented. The winter weather is cold and Christmas has been observed as a religious festival but with none of the traditional celebrations as we're all still in mourning for Henry. Other than the traditional feast for the benefit of the servants it's a quiet time.

With the harsh snowfalls of January painting the landscape white, Robert uses what little daylight there is sitting by the window and reading while Amy sews. They're expecting Robert Blount to ride from London with news of business transactions to be made, letters to be signed and accounts to be scrutinised but the deep snow has all but cut us off from any form of communication. Still our small family here at this mansion of Mr Hyde's is self sufficient. Many of the animals were slaughtered before Christmas and, as the nights became colder and the ponds froze over, the meat was preserved in pits of ice hewn from the ponds. Now we only have to feed the animals intended for breeding next spring and the three cows still producing a little milk. In the buttery there's plenty of cheese, ale, preserves, meat pickled in spices and jellies while in the grain store, guarded from the mice by a family of cats, there's wheat and rye for bread, dried peas and beans. We will not starve.

By mid February the days are longer and a short spell of good weather allows the outside world to reach us again. Mr Blount, ever the faithful servant to Lord Robert, battles through the mud and melting snow to reach us and brings astonishing news from the court.

Just after Christmas the Queen had convinced herself once again that she was expecting to give birth to a child although Prince Philip left her for Flanders five months ago and has not returned since. Mary's certain that during his stay in England, a stay of just three months, she had conceived an heir to the throne and was again begging him to return to court. But Philip mistrusted her assessment of the situation even though it was widely reported that, during his summer stay in England, they were enjoying a second honeymoon! And now he must be remembering with some embarrassment the previous debacle of Mary's "confinement" and refuses to return.

Robert gives a faint smile. "He had many mistresses in Flanders," he says. "I think Philip's enjoying his freedom too much." Amy gives him a sharp and quizzical look. If Philip had mistresses, what about those around him?

"Anyway," continues Blount, "The Queen is still adamant that she's with child though the word at court is that her swollen belly is a sign of something far worse, a much more serious illness. It's rumoured that," - Blount looks around to check there are no servants around - "she may well die before the year is out." To talk of the Queen's death is treason and we're all shocked. Blount leans back in his chair and smiles.

"Whatever," he continues, "There's even worse to tell. Calais has fallen to the French."

"What! Calais?"

"I'm afraid it's quite true. The French attacked the garrison there while everyone was still celebrating at the beginning of January. They took our men by surprise and the town fell after a short struggle."

"But we've held Calais for two hundred years. It was the last of our possessions in France. Why did the Spanish not come to our assistance?" says Mr Hyde.

"Obviously," says Blount, "They did not believe they had anything to gain now that they've made their peace with the French king. So now we have no English possessions in France at all."

"After all our sacrifices on their behalf," Robert muses sadly, obviously remembering how Henry died helping Philip and the Spaniards.

"The people in London are blaming the Queen and her Spanish blood for getting us into this plight. They're hungry too. After all the bad summer weather last year and this harsh winter, food is in short supply and people in the countryside are starving. Mary's spent all the money in the coffers on Prince Philip's wars and this, together with the persistent burnings of poor folk, is making her a figure of hate. Many will be glad to see her dead. They think that England's sorry state is a result of everything she's done and that she's angered God himself. They want an English queen with English blood in her veins."

"Elizabeth," says Amy flatly. Blount nods.

"And what about her mother, the whore Anne Boleyn? I thought many declare Elizabeth to be a bastard." Amy's feelings against the princess rise to the surface again.

"My lady wife! Hold your tongue! Think what you are saying and be grateful that you are among friends. Really, Amy, I sometimes doubt your judgement – you are such a foolish, gossiping, empty headed girl."

Amy blushes bright red at his rebuke and says nothing more.

"We have to think carefully what our next move will be," says Robert to Blount, "So please repeat nothing of what you've heard here." He glares at Amy. "Return to the city and let me know immediately if the Queen's health takes a further turn for the worse. We will stay here and do what we can to further our family's fortunes away from the court."

Blount nods. He knows what Robert means and so does Amy. Elizabeth's residence at Hatfield is only ten miles ride away.

But Robert and Amy do return to the city in the spring, staying at Christchurch and signing a legal document to raise money. The manor at Hales Owen is finally sold to Mr Forster.

"The money is so that we can find a manor in Norfolk," says Amy confidently. "Robert wants a huge deer park so that he can spend pleasant days out hunting."

I nod in agreement but my own assessment of the situation is rather different. Robert wants the money to provide Elizabeth with the wages for a small army of servants willing to fight on her behalf when the time comes. Lady Elizabeth, the Queen in waiting, is increasing her influence and power.

Chapter Eighteen
A New Queen

We spend the summer of 1558 at Throcking and, most surprisingly, Robert and Amy are indeed looking at properties in Norfolk. Today they're talking to Mr Flowerdew about the estate Amy inherited from her father and about a manor at Flincham which is close to Syderstone and has a manor house that is at least inhabitable!

Amy stands over Robert as he sits at the table and roles out the plans and drawings of Mr Flowerdew's survey. She can scarcely conceal her excitement. Robert, who's not been well over the summer, is still convalescing and is unable to visit Flincham for himself just yet and Amy's loved having him at home and all to herself. Their deliberations are interrupted by the sound of horses being ridden hard up to the driveway to Throcking manor.

Amy runs to the window. "It's Blount," she says, "And Verney's with him." She frowns. She doesn't like Richard Verney, another of Robert's drinking and gambling companions. "What do they want?"

We soon find out. Apparently the Queen has taken a turn for the worse, and suffers a high fever with sneezing and a racking cough. "She won't survive this," says Verney with a note of satisfaction.

"Sorry, my love, I have to leave," says Robert to Amy's incredulous look.

"You can't leave yet. You've not been well yourself. My Lord please do not risk your own health. Richard and Thomas will keep you informed – won't you?" she says, turning to appeal to them. They say nothing and Verney smiles that insolent smile that says, 'You are not in charge here, my lady; your wishes mean nothing to us.' Mr Hyde has just entered the chamber.

"Mr Hyde," says Amy desperately, "Please advise my Lord Robert against riding out. He wishes to travel to London to ascertain the state of the Queen's health at the risk to his own."

But Mr Hyde makes no comment either. Robert's already leaving, calling back to Amy, "My Lady Amy, you must not interfere. These are matters of which you know nothing. You must leave me to be the judge of this."

Amy sinks into the chair that Robert's just vacated and Mr Flowerdew rolls up the plans.

"I'll leave these with you, my Lady. Mr Hyde will take good care of them and maybe we can resume our discussions upon Lord Robert's return." He takes his leave talking to Mr Hyde about trivial matters, the price of wool, the harvest, the state of the countryside – all irrelevant in Amy's view – and we two are left alone.

"Robert didn't even say where he was going," wails Amy. "I expect it's to Christchurch so he can be close to the Queen." I don't say anything but I am certain that, from now on, Robert will be setting his sights on Mary's successor.

Summer turns into autumn and, to Amy's surprise, Robert is back again at Mr Hyde's house even though he now makes frequent trips to unspecified destinations. Mary had seemed to be recovering from her illness but has again relapsed, this time with her old complaint, and it seems that the Queen, broken hearted by Philip's apparent disinterest and lack of affection for her, has accepted the fact that she's dying. The level of activity at Throcking intensifies whether Robert is here or not and there are frequent visitors we have never seen before. We take to eaves dropping to gain more information.

It seems that the Queen has not yet named her successor and Elizabeth has moved from Hatfield, two miles to the north, to the fortified residence at Brocket Hall, ready to defend her claim to the throne. She's preparing for a fight. As October turns into November the roads to Hatfield become busier and busier with people flocking to show their allegiance to the woman they believe will be the next queen. Elizabeth has been well prepared for this moment, it seems, and has many gentlemen retainers prepared to help her defend her claim, not even counting those who are happy to serve her without financial reward but in anticipation of her recognition and favour in years to come. And both Amy and I know that Robert is prominent among this group. Elizabeth will be relishing every moment.

"I know Robert will send for me soon so we can both be at court together when the new queen accedes to the throne," says Amy. "He'll always want me by his side. Things have changed now. He's still ambitious, yes, but now I'm part of his ambition. After the disastrous events in Flanders he saw the benefit of a settled family life and now he wants us to be together all the time – well, nearly all the time. He'll have to spend time at court, of course, and I may not always be with him but he'll always come back to me, as he does now."

Amy's comments lack conviction and Robert's visits to Throcking become less and less frequent, to my great concern. When he does come, it's usually for some urgent meeting and not to see his wife. Then he's away again. It seems to me just like a return to the old days when the Dudley family's ambition was limitless.

The matter's settled in November when Robert comes once more to Mr Hyde's house for a fleeting visit.

"Right, my Lady," says Robert striding through the Great Hall in his riding attire, "Events are moving fast now. Mary's close to death and has sent the Spanish ambassador to meet Princess Elizabeth with the news that the succession is to be determined by their father's will ……. and since Henry, our noble Prince, decided that Mary would be succeeded by Elizabeth in the event of Mary being without issue, all is set for a smooth change. However there are some who wish Elizabeth ill and would prefer to see her Catholic cousin, Mary Stuart, on the throne. Since we cannot tell where this may lead, it will be safer if I move you and your household to Lincoln where you will be far away from any fighting or, I shudder to say, civil war or invasion from France."

"Lincoln!" Amy is speechless. "But I thought you said that all would go smoothly once the succession was decided by Queen Mary."

"There will be no arguing, my Lady. The future, and *our* future, depends on far more than your frivolous thoughts and wishes. I have made all the necessary arrangements with friends. You will travel to Lincoln tomorrow."

With this he leaves us, striding back down the hall where Mr Hyde is waiting in the doorway. From the window Amy and I can see the two men talking

150

earnestly while the groom brings Robert a new horse. With a wave to his friend, Amy's husband gallops away in the direction of Hatfield.

Two weeks later we're in Lincoln and there's a tremendous commotion in the streets. People are running and shouting and the church bells are ringing. The news has reached us this far north that Queen Mary is dead and that Elizabeth is our new Queen. Throngs of people appear from nowhere, all laughing and celebrating, tables are set up in the street and folk carry out of their houses whatever they can spare, a ham, a pie, a loaf of bread, some butter and cheese and flagons of ale.

Poor Mary! There will be no mourning for the Queen, once welcomed as the rightful heir, now hated and despised for bringing England to the brink of ruin. The only person with a very long face – and it's not on account of Mary – is my friend Amy.

Chapter Nineteen
A Different Kind of Life

In Lincoln we hear all manner of things about Elizabeth's triumph and nothing is to Amy's liking. Elizabeth has allowed a brief period to elapse (to show a dignified respect for her sister!) before making her triumphant journey into London. People report how the new Queen looked everywhere to catch the admiring glances of the crowd, smiling at some, speaking graciously with others and waving at the cheering onlookers. She was in no hurry and ready to savour the moment to the full. Riding immediately behind her, clothed in rich and splendid attire, was her new equerry, Master of the Queen's Horse, Robert Dudley.

"So rebellion was avoided then," says Amy, disconsolately and unnecessarily.

"It would appear so – but this is merely the beginning and we must look to the future to see what will happen next. After all there will be no more moments like this. It's a one-off and Robert will have to remember that he too has a family life to attend to." I'm trying to look on the bright side for Amy's sake.

"No, Kat, I think not. This is what he's always wanted. He and Elizabeth have been the best of friends since childhood and she'll come to depend on him more and more. As Master of the Horse he'll always need to be there, organising pageants and royal progresses, ensuring that the Queen has the best hunting parties and riding out with her. Already I'm a widow."

"No, no, dear Amy. Lord Robert loves you and will not desert you, just you wait and see." I try to put as much conviction as I can into these sentiments.

By Christmas Lord Robert has sent his men to take us back to Throcking.

"My Lady Amy welcome back, welcome back," says Mr Hyde. "Your dear husband, our Lord Robert, has been especially chosen by the Queen to be at her side during the festivities. How you and your kin are favoured. It must be wonderful for you to know that your dear Lord is so favoured."

"Yes, indeed it is, Mr Hyde. You are most kind and I'm sure that your kindness will be long remembered by my Lord."

Mr Hyde smiles and bows obsequiously and leaves. Three servant girls enter with some spiced wine and little cakes.

"Oh Lady Amy," says one coyly, "Your Lord Robert is held in great esteem by the Queen and people say he leaves her not, day and night, so determined is he that she will have a prosperous start to her reign."

"Yes and they say that she is so pleased to have such a noble Lord accompanying her that she made him her Master of the Horse so that he should always be there," says another.

"They say that he went to congratulate her on the day of the old Queen's death and looked so handsome and dashing on his white stallion that Elizabeth almost swooned to see him thus."

"They say that Lord Robert and the Queen are inseparable. They make each other laugh and the ambassadors complain that England will be run by a group of young people who will do as they choose."

"Well," retorts Amy through gritted teeth in a smiling face, "I thank you all for your views on the subject. I am sure that it will be a change to see England governed in a more light hearted way and in a spirit of generosity. And," she says turning towards the one who made the comments about the Master of the Horse, "When I need some knowledge about my husband's appointments I am sure I will not have to ask a common serving girl. But thank you for your information – albeit news that is already weeks old. And I wish to remind you all that England is governed by the Queen and her Lord Secretary, William Cecil, and her advisors like Thomas Parry – and *not* by my poor kin. Moreover, if I hear you once more gossiping about my husband and the Queen, I will report your insolence to Mr Hyde and you will all be looking for positions in a new household."

Phew! The servant girls go bright red, curtsey to Amy and walk out much subdued.

"They did that on purpose."

"What?"

"Curtsey. They were mocking me."

"No, Amy, I don't think they were. I think that they knew they'd gone too far by trying to find out how much you knew and they were afraid for their positions in the household which they thought they might lose if you were angry with them. They're just silly empty headed girls."

"But if this is what they are saying to my face, Kat, then what is everyone saying behind my back?"

There's nothing I can say to this.

"I'll be glad," says Amy wearily, "When Robert asks me to join him at court. That will silence the gossips."

But Christmas has gone and still Amy has still not been invited to join her husband at court. Lord Robert says he is very busy with the task of planning the Queen's Coronation which is to take place on January 16th so there will be no time for him to travel north to Hertfordshire. We are left to imagine what the Christmas festivities have been like at the Queen's residence at Whitehall and what part Amy's husband has played in the celebrations. Elizabeth loves dancing and Robert is an athletic dancer!

Throcking Manor was merry this year with dancing and music, story telling and masques – all the kinds of thing that Amy would normally revel in. Yet I haven't seen her smile for many weeks. She received presents from her husband, delivered by his henchmen, a gold chain and some pretty gold buttons for her gown. She examined them carefully, unsmiling and thoughtful, and I could read her mind; she was wondering what Robert had bought for the Queen and whether his presents to Elizabeth were much more extravagant.

In January she receives a letter from her husband with the news from court. Elizabeth has given Robert, as a Christmas present, a gilt cup and a mansion at Kew not far from the Palace of Sheen where Robert and Amy were married almost nine years ago. Amy also discovers that Elizabeth spent her first nights in London in Somerset House, Amy and Robert's former home! This reminds my friend of the dresses she was forced to leave behind when we fled the city as traitors!

Finally, in March, another letter brings a piece of news that should make Amy rejoice but doesn't; Robert is to be made a Knight of the Garter, the highest honour his sovereign can confer upon him but this piece of news is to be kept a secret as Elizabeth has not yet made her decision official. The announcement will be made on St George's Day as is customary. Robert, however, then delights Amy by saying that first he intends to spend Easter at Throcking.

"There you are," I say, "He was just waiting until all the business of the coronation was out of the way. Now he misses you and wants to join you soon."

"But I thought the Garter Knights were all noblemen from ancient families," says Amy, "So why has Robert been singled out by the queen to receive such an honour. Both his father and his uncle were traitors and stripped of their membership of the Order of Knights of the Garter."

"It will be for everything he did preparing for her coronation. Robert always works hard as you know and, by all accounts, the coronation went smoothly with no hiccoughs. No wonder Elizabeth decided to reward him."

Secretly I'm worried – I have to reassure Amy, who hasn't been well and is suffering from her old problem, usually brought on by worry, but I'm very concerned for her. The gossip among the servants is that Amy's husband is the Queen's favourite and that the two of them are never far apart.

But what can Elizabeth do? Robert is a married man and even the Queen cannot take another woman's husband. Can she?

Robert arrives at Easter with everything that's necessary to make the occasion a memorable one, entertainers and musicians, cooks, wonderful food and spices for the feasting and a host of admiring followers. His clothes are the finest money can buy, a declaration of his elevated position at court; he's certainly been catapulted to fame and he's revelling in his new found success.

But, when he leaves a few days later, Amy's disappointed that her husband hasn't been more loving towards her. Indeed he's almost ignored her presence in the house, staying up late into the night, drinking and playing cards with his men and with Mr Hyde and finally collapsing into bed in his own chamber. She wants for nothing now as Robert ensures that all our needs are met and that we can all live well at Throcking. The only missing ingredient is love. Lord Robert no longer shows any real affection for his wife.

Amy's health deteriorates especially when she thinks that she's not to be invited to Robert's investiture as a Garter Knight, set to take place in early June at the castle of Windsor. She's depressed and, I fear, has heard the many rumours that are circulating about her husband's relationship with the Queen and that are now becoming common knowledge. Robert, hearing of his wife's condition, ensures that his physician sends her certain potions to ease her pain.

Amy's illness takes a dramatic turn when she begins to vomit. She can hardly keep a meal down and is becoming quite thin. As usual she doesn't hesitate to voice her concerns.

"I'm being poisoned. I am sure of it. I've never felt this way in my whole life," Amy tells Mr and Mrs Hyde, who look at each other in horror.

"My dear Lady Amy," says Mr Hyde, "You must not say such things. You will bring my house and my family into disrepute if you maintain that you are being poisoned by the food I serve. I beg you - take care to eat only those broths which agree with you as, it seems to me, you have a malady of the stomach caused by your other illnesses."

Back in the privacy of our chamber Amy's furious. "I *am* being poisoned Kat. I don't know who's responsible but I have never, never felt so ill in my whole life. What can I do? I have to eat but someone is putting something into my food."

"Try not to be so fearful," I reassure her. "From now on I'll go down to the kitchen and prepare your food myself. That will enable us to make a clear decision about your predicament. Nothing will pass your lips that I have not prepared with my own hand and I'll even taste it first."

So it is that I teach myself the art of cookery, cutting the meat to make Amy a broth that she may find appetising and safe and baking her bread myself.

"Don't forget the Lady Amy's powder," says one of the servants, regarding me with a mixture of amusement and disdain.

Lady Amy's powder! The medicine sent by Robert's own physician and delivered by the man Amy most distrusts, Richard Verney! The powders are kept in a locked cabinet and I have to ask for the key. Taking care not to be seen I remove the lot and slip them into my apron pocket, relocking the cabinet and putting the key in my pocket alongside the powders. Later the key will be missed but I can claim that I left it by the cabinet and that it must have fallen to the ground and been brushed away with the floor sweepings. For the first time in many days Amy has broth with no added medicine.

Later that night I slip down the stairs and light a candle in the kitchen. I take the folds of paper, each of which contains Amy's powdered medication, and empty the contents on the floor, sweeping the powder around with a brush to disperse it. I find a jar of flour which I mix with a little powdered gypsum I bought from an old woman who sells herbs and potions in the village and I carefully measure out a little into each paper, folding it closed again. Then I put the new papers of 'medicine' back into the cabinet, locking it, dropping the key onto the floor and kicking it into a corner where I will pretend to discover it in the morning. I extinguish the candle and make my way back up the stairs lit by the moonlight shining through the window.

Within a few days Amy's feeling much better. So much better that we arrange to visit friends of her brother who live in Suffolk accompanied, as always now, by the ever watchful Thomas Blount. In late May, back at Throcking Manor, Amy delightedly receives the news that she's invited to Christchurch, the house Robert uses in London.

"It's so I can travel with him to Windsor," says Amy joyfully, "For the Garter ceremony. Kat, I'm so happy. I knew he wouldn't forget me and that all the talk about Robert and Elizabeth was false. It's the start of a new life for us." Amy flings her arms round me and does a little dance.

Thomas Blount looks on with a half smile.

Chapter Twenty
A Disappointment

Robert sends his servants to transport the whole of Amy's household from Throcking Manor to London. Mr Hyde walks with us to our baggage train and helps us both into the first litter. We're travelling in style as befits the wife of a leading courtier and her retinue.

"Well …. Goodbye my Lady and you too, Mistress Katherine. Fare you well and God bless you," says Mr Hyde stiffly.

"Thank you kindly, Mr Hyde" says Amy happily, "We are indeed fortunate and I'm sure that Milord Robert will not forget your help and loyalty to all of us."

Mr Hyde bows in acknowledgement of the compliment.

"But where is Mrs Hyde," continues Amy, oblivious to the formality of Hyde's parting words.

"She is, er ……, somewhat indisposed," says Hyde embarrassed, "But she sends you her best wishes and says God speed. She says that she hopes we will all meet again some day."

"All we, who live in the belief that Christ Jesus will save us, will indeed meet again," says Amy brightly.

"Indeed," says Mr Hyde formally, "And now, God speed."

I can't help noticing that this departure is different from previous ones. There are no little cakes, preserves and savouries to eat on the journey and Mrs Hyde has given us a cold shoulder. Mr Hyde is more remote and less affectionate towards us and is behaving as if this will be our final visit to his home.

Amy seems to think that this means that he expects her to have a life at court from now on but, to me, it suggests something else. It suggests that Amy's accusations of poisoning have stung Mr Hyde deeply and he has requested that someone else take responsibility for the health of 'Milord Robert's wife' - hence the lack of provisions for the journey. I hope I'm wrong.

We depart from Throcking and three days later, having stayed at the best inns, arrive at Christchurch. When the carriages roll into the courtyard Amy expects to see Robert rushing out to greet her but he's not there. She sweeps into the Great Hall.

"Where is my Lord Robert?" she demands imperiously. The servants regard each other fearfully. Sir Richard Verney steps forward and sneers at the omnipresent Blount. Turning to Amy, he says unsmilingly, "He's gone to his home in Kew, my Lady .... to await his installation as a Garter Knight."

"But when are we to join him?" asks a bewildered Amy.

"You will not join him. Lord Robert was very unwell before he departed. He had a fever and wished to retire to the countryside to recover before the ceremony. He says you are to wait for him here."

"But if he's ill I must join him. It's a wife's duty to be beside her husband at such times."

Blount and Verney exchange a knowing look. "He said you were to stay here." Verney then says maliciously, "I am sure Lord Robert will find other solace and comfort at Kew to assist his recovery." Blount stifles a laugh.

161

"Was there no note, no letter from my Lord?" Amy is pathetic in her unwillingness to accept the situation for what we all know it to be.

The answer is simple. "No. He left no note."

Chapter Twenty One
A New Amy

To my surprise Robert does return to Christchurch –
clearly Elizabeth has let him off the leash for a time.
But it can't last as he has to arrange the Queen's first
summer progress when he'll be expected to
accompany her, hunt with her and dine with her at all
times. He makes frequent journeys to court but only
once taking Amy with him when he was sure that she
and Elizabeth wouldn't meet. When he returns to
Christchurch he stays up late into the night, drinking
and gambling with his henchmen.

Amy loved her visit to court and came back with
tales of how she met this person and that person.

"I met Mr Cecil today, Kat. I haven't seen him
since Robert and I married at Sheen. My, he's grown
so important now but he was very kindly towards me.
And so was the Spanish ambassador. He said that he
was sorry to hear that I hadn't been well but was
pleased to see that I'm now much recovered. I told
him that I was being very careful to eat only foods
that agree with me and he smiled and kissed my hand
and said that I was very sensible. He's so charming.
He said Lord Robert was lucky to have such a
beautiful wife."

Unfortunately Amy's run of good health seems to
break after only two weeks at Christchurch and she's
once again wracked with pains and vomiting. Worse
still Robert, one night, comes home from court
dressed completely in black.

"Robert," gasps Amy, weakly, "What's
happened? Has someone died? Oh dear I hope it's
not someone I know."

Robert turns on his heel, as if surprised to find her awake and alert, and walks out, slamming the door behind him. Alarm bells sound in my head. It's time to act and act quickly but what to say to Amy? It's best to be straightforward.

"My dear Amy," I venture, "It's obvious that someone somewhere wishes you ill and out of the way. No, you mustn't look at me like that! Robert was dressed in black because he was expecting to find you much worse than you are. Or – he was dressed so because he's been told to frighten you into feeling that you're dying. And we both know who would be behind such a mean trick …. the same person who gives him his orders. Your symptoms are exactly the same as they were at Throcking Manor. So I'll prepare your food as I've done before and I'm sure you'll recover. Meanwhile you must ask Lord Robert if we can spend the time when he is away on the royal progress at your cousin Scott's house in Camberwell. He can hardly say no without being implicated in a plot against you and you'll be safe there."

Amy's face is a picture of misery. "I think the same, Kat. From now on I must think about my own preservation and I'm coming to the conclusion that Robert no longer loves me. They're hunting me down, Kat – Robert's men – I'm sure of it and I'm now certain that, if he knows about it – which he must - he doesn't care. You're right. I'll be safe at John's house."

Lord Robert doesn't express any emotion in his dark, fathomless, black eyes when Amy asks him if she can go to her cousin's house to recover. I'm struck by the fact that his eyes are so much like Elizabeth's; the Queen is shortsighted and peers

164

through expressionless black orbs in order to see well. Now Robert stares at Amy with an inscrutable gaze and it's hard to judge what's going on in his mind. But his attention is focused on the forthcoming progress anyway so he accedes to Amy's wish.

Under my care Amy starts to grow strong again and, as Robert and the Queen relish the prospect of a long summer progress in each other's company, we make our way quietly to John Scott's peaceful home south of the river.

Amy's been very quiet and deep in thought during the short journey. Now she confides in me. "From now on, Kat, I will place no demands on my Lord. I will not cause trouble and there'll be no more arguments over Elizabeth. Instead I'm going to make certain that Robert keeps me in luxury. I'll order whatever fine gowns I wish and he will pay for them and in return he can have his friendship with the Queen, much good may it do him. I'll have a comfortable life and he can have his Elizabeth. I pity him. She'll soon tire of him and spit him out when some handsome foreign prince courts her. The Spanish ambassador told me she has many royal suitors all across the world. What has Robert got that foreign princes could not give her twenty times over and more besides? And what's more they don't have wives waiting for them at home. She'll never be truly his because he's married to me. Robert already has a wife."

And that's precisely what troubles me and makes me feel uneasy for my friend.

Chapter Twenty Two
Eavesdroppers

We spend three whole weeks with Amy's cousin, John Scott, and his family. The house and gardens are delightful at this time of year with scents of lavender, thyme and rosemary drifting across the warm still air of the summer evenings. Amy's well again and once more enjoying the admiring company of the young members of the family. Young Thomas, who was a small boy when we last saw him, is now a young man of thirteen.

"Tell me about the court, Lady Amy, if you please. Does everyone there walk around in cloth of gold? Do they ride white horses when they go out to hunt and can they eat marzipan whenever they please?" Thomas is particularly fond of marzipan!

"Well, Thomas, the people there wear ordinary clothes just as we do but the palaces are very cold so they wear furs quite a lot and their skirts and cloaks have fur linings but only the Queen is allowed to wear ermine. And as for the food – they drink a lot of wine and eat a lot of meat, as much as they please, and have marzipan made into the shapes of flowers and animals or even toy palaces made entirely of marzipan."

Thomas' eyes go wide. "And the horses! What about the horses?"

"Oh yes, I was forgetting that, Thomas; they have the most beautiful horses because my husband and your cousin, Lord Robert, chooses them himself for the Queen to ride."

"What does she look like, Amy," says Thomas, forgetting his manners.

At this point Amy goes red and changes the subject for which I'm quite relieved. I'd wondered what her description of Elizabeth would be!

One evening, while we are taking in the night air in the silent gardens sitting lost in thought on a bench which encircles a great tree, we hear the latch on the house door clatter shut. There are men's voices coming in our direction. Whoever it is has obviously stopped behind the tree and cannot see us.

"She did. She did it. She kept that popish whore Dormer, Feria's wife, standing for most of the afternoon."

"What the Spanish Ambassador's wife – Jane Dormer?"

"Well – he's not ambassador now; De la Quadra is. Feria's gone home to Spain and his English whore's following him. Our Elizabeth didn't want popish ladies-in-waiting about her."

I recognise the lewd voice of Sir Richard Verney and the fawning tones of Thomas Blount. Amy looks at me with a horrified expression. What are they doing here?

"But Feria's wife's expecting their first child," says Blount.

"Yes, you should have seen the size of her! She was as big as a Spanish galleon. The Spaniards were outraged and offered Dormer a chair but she refused. She didn't want to offend the Queen by sitting down so she stood and waited and waited and waited ….."

There's the hideous sound of Verney's loud guffawing.

"So what happened?" inquires Blount.

"Oh someone, probably Cecil, warned the Queen that she'd cause a diplomatic incident if the Count de

Feria's wife collapsed and lost the child; so she relented and invited Dormer in for her farewell audience."

"Was there a quarrel?"

"No – apparently they were both very lady-like and well behaved. They laughed and joked and wished each other well!" Verney sneers the words.

"And My Lord Robert ... was he there?" says Blount curiously.

"No, but when I told him he threw his head back and roared with laughter. 'That's my Elizabeth,' he said, 'She knows how to play them. What a clever woman she is.' And he strode off to find his lady love to congratulate her."

Amy's as still as one of those marble statues they have in Italy and just as white. We continue to sit motionless and unseen in the gathering darkness.

Blount then resumes the conversation, "Well I expect Jane Dormer deserved it. Her husband can't stand Elizabeth, that's why he's quitting. He thinks her reign will end in tears and there'll be a rebellion against our Lord Robert when she marries him. Rumour has it that Feria's wife's been trying to smuggle Jane Grey's sister out of the country so she can marry a Spanish Hapsburg."

"What? Katherine Grey? Now there's a flighty little piece!"

Blount laughs. "She certainly is. But, after Elizabeth, she has as good a claim to the throne as Mary Stuart. And what's more she's not a Scottish Frenchwoman like the Queen of Scots. If there's a rebellion against Elizabeth and Robert, the Spanish are planning to bring 'Queen' Katherine and her Hapsburg husband back to England."

"Who told you all this?"

"Oh Lord Robert has a whole army of spies! He'll be ready for this when the time comes."

"You mean when he marries Elizabeth?"

"Quite. I think it's perhaps time we went back in. We've a long day ahead of us tomorrow. William Chauncey's organising everything for the move to your place from Christchurch. Has all the household of 'Milord Robert's lady' " (he says this in a mocking sing song tone of voice) "been sent to Compton Verney?"

"Yes everything set off from Christchurch this morning including that idiotic fool of a woman, Picto. They should arrive at Compton Verney in three days' time."

We sit in stunned silence as the voices fade and we hear the sound of the door slamming, making us rise quickly to our feet.

"Compton Verney! That's Richard Verney's manor," gasps Amy in a shocked voice. "Why are we going there, Kat? It's in Warwickshire and miles from court. I don't want to go."

Neither do I but it seems we'll have little choice. "Quickly Amy," I say, "Back inside before the door is bolted. Your cousin John doesn't know we're out here."

Back in our chamber we talk well into the night. The gentle Jane Dormer and her husband, the Count de Feria, were universally liked and indeed he'd advised Queen Mary not to pursue her path of violence. The burning of the Protestants had sickened him but ultimately he was powerless to stop Mary's over-zealous religious fervour. The Count dislikes Elizabeth and now, seeing no future for himself and his modest English wife at court, he's resigned his post as ambassador so that they can both retire to Spain and raise their family there. Elizabeth had thus behaved disgracefully towards Jane when the latter went to make her farewells.

"She's like that you know – Elizabeth. She only wants her own cronies around her and lots of men admiring her. She despises all other women and especially me because she wants Robert. But she won't have him, Kat. Over my dead body, she won't have him. He's besotted with her now but she can't marry him. We Dudleys are despised and detested by many. Even if he divorces me the nobility won't let her marry him. She'll have to find a foreign prince to wed and then I'll have him back."

"But I won't go with anyone to Compton Verney unless I have a letter from my Lord instructing me to do just that," she continues. "Why should I?"

So the talk goes on well into the night. By morning we're both worn out and completely unfit for a long journey. I haven't slept at all and the thought that I can't get out of my head is this. If Verney and Blount hadn't seen two shadowy figures sitting underneath the tree then they must have been blind. Given that, they must have known that Amy could hear the whole conversation. Did they want her to hear about Robert's plans to marry the Queen and weren't they afraid that Robert might disapprove of their actions? Just what are they trying to do?

Chapter Twenty Three
Compton Verney

No we didn't argue with Blount and Verney. Or demand to see written proof that we were to go with them. We simply got into the carriage like two obedient well dressed dolls and set off for Warwickshire.

It was a three day journey, largely spent in silence. When we could be sure that no one could overhear there were short attempts at stilted conversation conducted in a monotone on Amy's part.

"She swears, you know, and uses oaths." I don't need to ask who is the subject of Amy's thoughts.

"Does she?"

"Yes. Robert always used to correct me if my speech was not completely dignified. He didn't like any imperfection in me, not even if I, quite rightly, criticised the way a woman was dressed or complained about any of our gentlewomen companions."

"Well, that's men for you. They expect their wives to be beyond reproach."

"They say she lies in her bed and then walks around in her shift all morning. They say even passers-by can see her breasts when she leans out of the window. How can a woman behave in such a slovenly way? I can't imagine what Robert sees in her."

I can. She's the Queen and he's ambitious.

When we reach Compton Verney we're greeted very cordially and are pleasantly surprised. Warwickshire is a beautiful county and the manor house is large and well appointed. All the local gentlewomen are waiting to welcome our arrival and Amy is feted as if she were a royal personage. She's very surprised!

Unfortunately everyone, from the lowliest servant to the highest ranking lady, is talking about Amy's husband and some of the talk is not what Amy wanted to hear.

"We hear that, on the progress, the Queen so requires your husband's opinion on all things that he is never far from her ….. day and night."

"Is it true, Lady Dudley, that the Queen is as good at hunting as any man and that your husband is hard pressed to find horses fast enough for her?"

"Yes, my Lady, they say she hunts all day and none of the courtiers can keep up with her, except your husband. She must have great courage and be an excellent horsewoman."

"Apparently at the castle of the Earl of Arundel the Queen and Sir Robert sit at banquets side by side and laugh and dance until it is time for bed."

And so on and so on. Amy smiles around as all the questions and comments are fired in her direction and is lost for words. Finally I have to put an end to the chatter.

"I am sure there'll be time to talk to my Lady Amy in the days to come and meanwhile shall we all go into the Great Hall? I heard someone say that dinner is about to be served and we are weary with travelling and would like to go to our beds early."

The dinner is a huge banquet but not on the scale of the one that the Queen and Amy's husband will be enjoying at the expense of the Earl of Arundel. All the gossip points to the fact that Elizabeth and Robert are in the middle of one long party and having a wonderful time. Amy has heard the rumours and is quiet and thoughtful throughout the meal.

"I hope that all this rumour and scandal will stop soon," Amy says resignedly when we go up to bed. "You would think that people would be more tactful towards me. And Robert's obviously making a fool of himself. She can't marry him and is thus using him as her plaything until she finds someone more suitable. Dear Jesus, Kat! If this is what they are saying in the Warwickshire countryside what will they be saying in the courts of Europe?"

What indeed!

The weeks pass by and the Royal Progress is over. Amy half expects her husband to join her at Compton Verney but she receives a letter from him stating that the Queen is ill again and he cannot leave her side. Elizabeth, he says, has few friends she can depend upon at such times and has asked him not to leave her. Amy quietly tears the note into tiny pieces and, later that evening, throws it onto the fire.

Amy's very careful about what she eats at Compton Verney. She chooses only the food that others have taken first from the same platter. And we never eat alone. Richard Verney is as insultingly obsequious as ever and we spend as little time in his company as is possible, given that he is our host. The chattering women, seeing that they cannot persuade Amy to make any comment on the subject of her husband, soon realise that they have nothing to gain by waiting on us at Compton Verney and we are mercifully left to our own devices.

Then another letter arrives from Lord Robert. He has been made Lord Lieutenant of Warwickshire along with a local man, Sir Ambrose Cave, and

Amy's half brother, John Appleyard, has been made Sheriff of Norfolk by the Queen, much to the annoyance of the Duke of Norfolk who thought that the appointment should have been under his control and who detests Robert Dudley! Amy's both delighted and puzzled. This is an unexpected honour for her brother but she doesn't dwell on it too much as, reading further, she's pleased to learn that Robert would now like to buy a manor house in Warwickshire since it was his family seat in days gone by.

But I'm puzzled over her brother's sudden catapult to fame in Norfolk. Why would Elizabeth favour Amy's kin?

My suspicious mind harbours thought that I can't mention. If Robert is planning to divorce Amy, which he could well do since, after almost ten years of marriage, they have no children, then winning Amy's brothers over to his side would well suit his purpose. If this is the case then Amy's truly alone.

Verney's men do not spare Amy's feelings as they discuss Robert and Elizabeth's relationship within her earshot. The latest piece of gossip is that the two of them have played a huge joke on the Imperial Ambassador and have used Robert's sister, Mary Sidney, as their unsuspecting accomplice. Apparently Mary was furious when she discovered how she had been used by them both and is now not speaking to Robert.

The story goes that, fearing an attack from the French and their newly crowned king and queen, Francis and Mary Queen of Scots, Elizabeth called Mary Sidney to the presence chamber and told her to go to Bruener, the Imperial Ambassador, and tell him

174

that she was ready to consider a marriage with the Archduke Charles, son of the Holy Roman Emperor. Mary believed Elizabeth and did this in all good faith. When Bruener tried to broach the subject with Elizabeth, she, the Queen, merely played for time by wavering in her resolve to marry and, when the threat from the French had passed, Elizabeth was downright rude in her dismissal of the Ambassador.

"She's like that," says Amy when we discuss this latest piece of news for the sixth time. "She thinks she can do what she likes."

"Well – she can, can't she? She's the queen and no one can tell her what to do." I have no advice to offer my friend.

"She'll have to be careful. She'll have the reputation of being the whore of the continent soon, as her mother did." There's grim satisfaction in Amy's voice.

We both look round hastily to see if anyone has been listening. It's nearly the end of November and the wind is howling around Compton Verney but we're completely alone. "Where's Richard Verney?" asks Amy suddenly.

I have no information to provide on that subject either. We haven't seen him for four days now, not since he learned that the position of constable of Warwick Castle, which he had asked Lord Robert to give to him, had been given to someone else, someone whom Robert had evidently decided was more suitable. Before he left we found the little dove that came to take bread crumbs from Amy's hand lying outside the dove-cote with its neck broken. It was, as Verney would have put it, a 'casual thing', meaning that he considered its death to be of no

175

consequence, but for us it was a little joy in this sad world that had been taken away. And God knows that Amy has little joy these days.

Almost as if Amy had had a premonition, there's the sound of horsemen in the courtyard. Looking through the window we can see the stable lads helping Verney and his men to dismount. As they lead the sweating horses to the stable, the men follow Verney as he strides into the house ripping off his riding gauntlets. He's clearly in a bad mood.

Amy starts to shake visibly at the sound of boots on the wooden stair and gives me a frightened look. The door's flung open and Sir Richard marches over to Amy who cowers before him. But at the table he stops and flings down a letter.

"From 'Milord Robert'," he sneers. "I take it that you've not been very happy during your stay here, despite my generous hospitality."

Amy shakes her head in denial; she's bewildered.

"Anyway," continues Verney, "You will soon be rid of my loathsome presence. Your Lord has been made Lieutenant of Windsor Castle and wishes you and your family to move to the house of a friend of his in Oxfordshire so that you'll be closer together - like two turtle doves," he adds with another sneer. His men laugh.

When they've left, Amy turns to me and says, "When have I ever said that I'm not happy here, Kat? Who has said this? Richard Verney must be guessing that I've written to Lord Robert and yet I haven't."

I'm just as puzzled. It's true that Sir Ambrose Cave and his wife, with whom we've sometimes dined, have remarked on the fact that Amy is pale and unhappy but we've never complained to anyone. And who is this friend in Oxfordshire to whose house we are to be removed, bag and baggage. Secretly I rejoice as I've never trusted Sir Richard Verney and it seems that Robert is now sending out a message that he wants his wife closer to him. Maybe his affair with the Queen is cooling down which is good news for Amy.

My friend is busy reading Robert's letter with a delighted expression. We are, she tells me, going to Cumnor Place, a manor house near Abingdon which is rented by a well respected local man named Sir John Forster. We're to depart the following day.

As we prepare for the journey one of the grooms from the stable comes in with a serious and apologetic demeanor. Pavane, Amy's beloved mare now fifteen years old, has been found dead on the floor of her stall in the stable. It is not a good omen.

Chapter Twenty Four
Cumnor Place

We're clopping along a road that goes past Oxford
and thinking black thoughts. It's late November and
already there are flurries of snow in the cold wind
which whistles round our carriage. This is no time
for exploring the city, not that we'd want to do so.
It's only three years since the dreadful burnings of
Latimer, Ridley and Cranmer at the instigation of
Queen Mary. Amy has a horror of viewing the site
where they were burned, the ditch outside the city,
and won't even look in that direction. Besides she's
lost in her own thoughts again and wears a worried
frown. The sooner we reach Cumnor, the better.

"She was old I suppose."

"Who? Pavane?" I know where her thoughts lie.

"Yes. She was fifteen. She was five years old
when Robert gave her to me as a present, all those
years ago when we were happy and about to be
married. And yet," she continues, "She was in good
health and father had horses at Syderstone and
Stanfield that were twenty and still working well."

Amy ponders this and then gives a long sigh.
"It's no use. I expect we'll never know. It was a pity
we had to leave James behind at Mr Hyde's house.
He was a good groom, when he was sober, and would
have looked after her properly if he'd been with us.
At least he would have told me if he'd seen she was
ill and I would have had a chance to say goodbye to
her." A tear rolls down her face. "She was always so
kind to me. She never put a foot wrong. She looked
after me and I would have liked to say goodbye."

The tears are flowing fast now. This little mare had been devoted to Amy and she was the only connection to her husband and the once happy life they had. Now all that, the romance, the happiness and anxieties, the despair and the hope for the future are just a memory. Amy's in a state of nothingness, neither married nor unmarried, and all the time knowing that her once loving husband now has thoughts for no one except the Queen. I put my hand over hers; there's no consolation I can offer, either for the loss of her horse or for the loss of her husband.

"Do you think animals go to heaven, Kat? Everyone says they have no soul and cannot go."

"All I can say, Amy, is that heaven wouldn't be heaven for me without animals there. Not fighting animals like the pitiful bears that are prized only for their ability to tear at the poor dogs that are set against them in the pits - but a place where we can all live together in peace and safety."

"That's a very unusual idea, Kat. I don't think the church would agree with you and it's a good thing that Mary's not still alive. She would have had you burned as a witch with your animal familiars."

"Oh they aren't familiars. They don't talk to me and tell me what to do. It's the devil who puts wicked thoughts into people's minds not animals. I just think that they are so much like us, and we like them."

"Hush, Kat. Such talk may be construed as heresy. Say no more. You don't know who's listening." Amy drops her voice to a whisper.

The wind around the carriage blows even more ferociously making conversation difficult. It seems to me that the weather's getting worse. Winter starts early and goes on until well into the spring and we have rain all summer long. During Mary's reign the people blamed the bad weather and the harvest failures on Mary's burnings and many wished her dead. Elizabeth was a breath of fresh air for some. Well she's reigned for a year now and we hear that many at court find her behaviour disappointing. Rumour and gossip surround her and her favourite courtier, Robert Dudley. The worst is that Amy's husband and the Queen have adjoining bed chambers and visit each other day and night. It's common talk throughout the land and Amy must surely have heard such tittle-tattle.

The horses plough on through the wind and sleet and we pull our cloaks around us and huddle together. Then we begin to climb a hill and eventually someone shouts, "There it is!" and we both look up, eager to see our new dwelling place.

New! It's hardly that! An austere stone building lies ahead of us, completely unlike the pretty brick and timbered buildings of leafy Warwickshire. I have a feeling that Cumnor Manor, nesting in the lee of a ridge and facing towards Abingdon to the south, will be windy and bleak even in the height of summer. We've been told that it was once used by the monks in nearby Oxford as a summer residence, before King Henry's time when there were still monasteries. That is to say – before he met Elizabeth's mother, Anne Boleyn. Now it's a private dwelling place, owned by a Mr Owen, who was once a royal physician. The manor house is leased from him by Sir Anthony Forster, so our driver tells us. It's a strange place. There's no obvious front door!

The road winds up past a little church and along the north side of the building and, just as we're wondering where we will enter and who will be on hand to receive us, the driver guides the horses from the outer courtyard, under an archway in the building and into a central courtyard where a group of people are assembled, shivering in the cold. We guess that they haven't waited there all afternoon; a servant will have spotted our approach from an upper window.

A gentleman steps forward from the group and takes Amy's hand.

"My dear Lady Dudley – what a pleasure this is. Welcome to Cumnor and let us please go in, out of this cold wind."

"Thank you, Sir Anthony, I do hope that you've not been standing outside for long, waiting for me in such bad weather."

"No my dear lady, we came out when we saw your carriage approaching. I would like to show you round Cumnor but the weather will not allow it today ….. maybe one day when the wind is not so strong and cold."

We're ushered towards the Great Hall while the servants step forwards to take the baggage. The steaming, sweaty horses will be taken to the stables to be rubbed down with straw as no one wants them to get a chill and, as our driver manoeuvres them round the courtyard, we hear the sound of the remainder of our baggage train arriving on the road outside.

Inside the Hall there's a roaring fire piled high with logs and a long table spread with plates of all kinds of hot and freshly carved meat and the best manchet bread. Even Elizabeth will not fare better this evening and I secretly hope that Sir Anthony has not used a quarter of our winter rations on this extravagant display of hospitality. A servant pours huge cups of warm spiced wine. It's very sweet and welcoming and just to Amy's liking. Someone must have told Sir Anthony what my friend's food preferences are!

Our host then introduces us to the other occupants of Cumnor Place, starting with his wife, a shy and gentle lady. Then there is a Mrs Owen who is the mother of the man from whom Sir Anthony leases the house and another woman who is younger than the elderly Mrs Owen but older than Amy and me, a Mrs Odingsells. She is a gentlewoman companion to Mrs Owen. All the women are friendly and welcoming. Sir Anthony then summons a man called Bowes from the group of servants standing a little way off and tells Amy that this man will be her principal servant here and will attend to any errands for commodities she may require and will also take letters to and from her dear Lord, Sir Robert.

Finally Sir Anthony beams as he shows Amy the presents that Robert has sent to Cumnor to welcome her arrival, a jewelled looking glass and many yards of the finest blue sewing silk. Amy radiates pleasure to think that Robert has been so attentive to her needs and turns to the assembled women, including her servant Mrs Picto.

"What pleasant times we'll all have with our conversation and embroidery over the long winter months when we cannot walk outside in the garden. Thank you all for the welcome you have given me. I'm sure I will be very happy here."

The ladies are all pleased with the arrival of this new and eminent personage. Lady Dudley is going to be a welcome companion in the isolated little community of Cumnor.

The formalities over, we all sit down to a welcome and tasty dinner. Sir Anthony talks about his garden at Cumnor and how he likes to cultivate young plants in the spring; gardening is obviously something that he is passionate about. He describes the buildings that make up the Place and tells us that the archway, by which we entered the courtyard on our arrival, is underneath a Long Gallery. We can use this, when the weather is bad and we cannot ride out, to play skittles and to exercise, as it extends for the whole length of the house on its northern side. Sir Anthony is very sorry to hear of the death of Amy's riding horse and says that he will take great pains to find another sound and reliable palfrey when the spring arrives.

After our meal our host shows us to our chambers. Amy's are elegant and spacious in the south west corner, with enough room for her dresses and her waiting lady, Mrs Picto. The stairs up to Amy's bedchamber ascend in two flights with a 'landing' in between. From her outside doorway it's a just a stride through the inner courtyard to an archway in the wall which leads to the gardens and deer park. Sir Anthony says that he will be very pleased, in the warmer weather, to escort Lady Dudley around his well stocked terraced gardens.

My chamber is next to that of Mrs Owen and Mrs Odingsells while the Forsters and their servants sleep in the east wing of Cumnor Place. Between their bedchambers and mine is a chapel and, underneath the east wing, is another archway that leads into the churchyard of the tiny Cumnor church. All together, with the cellars, malting rooms and buttery, we could not have wished for a better place to spend the winter and we're delighted with the welcome we've been given.

Chapter Twenty Five
Christmas 1559

We've been at Cumnor for a month now and we've met most of the local gentry and dignitaries. Amy's something of a distinguished figure in the area and most of the women in the local community covet the opportunity to meet the wife of Sir Robert Dudley. With these meetings, however, comes the opportunity for court gossip relating to Amy's husband and the Queen, a situation which Amy naturally detests. It seems to be the main item of conversation at the moment as if no one can think of anything else and I'm amazed how insensitive even the kindest of our friends can be.

Time goes on but the gossip continues unabated. Sir Robert is the darling of all the ladies at court, they say, and Amy is so lucky to have such a charming husband. And she has no need to worry about his relationships with the ladies-in-waiting; the Queen will not allow his attention to wander beyond her own self …. nor his person either! The two of them are seldom apart, we are told in strictest confidence. Amy smiles and holds her tongue in public but, in the privacy of her chamber, she explodes.

"Well, it's nice to know what one's own husband is doing from the tongues of baggages and chattering jays! Really Kat, this is too much, too much to bear. Just wait til we next see Robert. I will remind him that he has his wife's sensitivities to think of and should curb his flirtatious nature." I nod in agreement but there's nothing I can say, no comfort to give.

However we are not entirely alone in our disapproval, entertaining as it may be to some. Some

185

of the Queen's most trusted companions and advisors have advised her in the strongest words against her continued relationship with Sir Robert. Needless to say the reckless and wilful Elizabeth has thrown all this advice back in their faces. She is the Queen; why should she take advice? She can do as she wishes.

Amy however is still convinced that Robert loves her, despite all the rumours flying around, and, although she doubts that he will be able to leave the court over the Christmas festivities, she truly believes that his heart is really with her and that it will not be long before he makes the thirty mile journey from Windsor to Cumnor to see her again, whether Elizabeth agrees or not.

Another piece of startling news is that Amy's husband is now so detested by members of the nobility at court that he's taken to wearing a chain mail vest underneath his fine clothes. He fears the assassin's dagger and the young Duke of Norfolk has stated openly that he would like to see Sir Robert dead and out of the way. They all think that the queen will never commit to a foreign or, for that matter, an English marriage while Robert is still hovering around her.

The news of the danger to Robert due to his foolhardy behaviour is very distressing to Amy, as are the occasional visits from Blount and Verney, but in the excitement of Christmas all the unpleasantness disappears. Sir Anthony has planned a wonderful season of entertainment for the ladies of Cumnor.

We spend Christmas day, as usual, praying and reflecting on the birth of our Saviour. All the folk from the local community assemble in Cumnor church and we're fortunate as we have only to walk across the courtyard and through an archway to be in the churchyard. We lift our gowns above our ankles and tiptoe over the snow-covered ground while poorer families arrive cold and with soaking wet feet after the walk up the hillside. Gentle folk and landowners travel to church in some style, the women in litters and the men on fine horses, and there is a collection of tethered horses and two carriages on the road outside Cumnor Place. Sir Anthony's men bring hay for the waiting animals while we inside are glad of the fur linings inside our gowns and cloaks. The church is very cold indeed.

A little wooden table stands at the back of the church, instead of the stone altar that stood in the middle of the chancel in Mary's time, all the paintings on the wall have been white washed out (which is a pity I think because I used to like to study them during the more tedious moments of the service) and there are no statues looking down on us and no ornaments on the altar - candlesticks and crucifixes are things of the past. When the priest blesses the wine (which we're now able to share with him) he reminds us that this is an act in remembrance of Christ's blood shed for us. These days we're told to believe that it doesn't actually change into the blood itself.

For the old folk of Cumnor you can see that this has taken a long time to get used to and they were far more comfortable with the old religion. Some of them linger after the service to look at the English Bible which is now a feature of every church in the land so that all we who can read can see the word of God for ourselves without the need to be a Latin scholar. To their delight and amazement Sir Anthony

187

reads to them from the gospels more of the story of the birth of Jesus.

The day after Christmas the festivities start with the giving of presents. Amy loves pretty things and shows child-like delight with her gifts from the Forsters and especially with her gift from Robert, a deep red velvet embroidered hood decorated with pearls. She wears it immediately and revels in the compliments she receives from Sir Anthony and Mrs Owen. Amy has a very pretty face when she's animated, something that did not escape the notice of the Spanish ambassador!

In the afternoon a group of travelling players arrives at Cumnor Place and the excitement mounts. At this time of year the days are very short and we're unable to sew or play cards for long in the evenings as our eyes get tired and sore in the dim candle light. An entertainment of music and story telling is something we all look forward to.

The five young men who form the troupe are all from nearby farms and villages. They bring musical instruments, a lute, a drum, a flute, a shawm and a recorder, and sing to the music they play. We know the tunes and never tire of them. One of the men is a local farmer, called Owain, who came originally from Wales. He is renowned for his stories of the Mabinogi, the amazing tales of the Welsh princes and the knights of King Arthur's court and Amy is enraptured as she listens intently. Sitting in the Great Hall with the older ladies of Cumnor, with Sir Anthony, with Amy's manservant, Mr Bowes, sent by Robert to deliver her letters and attend to her wishes, and with Mrs Picto, there's a calm warmth that makes us feel we're among friends. There's no sign of

Thomas Blount, who's presumably at court with Robert. Likewise the odious presence of Richard Verney, presumably celebrating Christmas at Compton Verney, is not missed by Amy!

The hall looks lush and green with all the tree branches brought in from outside. Holly and ivy decorate the walls, the lintels above the doors and the mantelpiece over the fireplace where the flames of a huge log fire leap and crackle casting long dancing shadows on the ceiling. On the cleanly swept floor the green rushes and evergreen branches give a gorgeous scent of warm pine all mixed with smells of rich cinnamon, cloves and spices. We're in a leafy grove, cosy and warm, settled and comfortable, and full of the special food reserved for Christmas treats.

The servants hand round little tartlets filled with sugared fruit and peel and flavoured with spice. The cook has even placed a tiny figure made of dough underneath each pastry lid to represent the Christ child asleep under his blanket. There's every kind of meat and savoury, an abundance of sweet wine and mead, candied preserved fruits, jellies and jams and, brought to Cumnor at great expense and especially for Amy, marzipan!

Everyone has been invited into the Hall to partake of the food, after we've had our fill, and to watch the entertainment, first the musicians and then the story tellers. The long table has been moved back and the servants are allowed to sit on it while we've seated ourselves beside the fire, Amy sitting on cushions on the floor, the skirts of her favourite russet taffeta gown spread prettily around her, her hair shining golden underneath the new French hood from Robert. I see the young men in the troupe gazing at

189

her for a little longer than perhaps they should and I cannot help thinking what a fool Robert Dudley is to throw away so rich a treasure.

The wine is sweet and intoxicating and the musicians are good. They play all our favourite tunes and even perform dances to some of them, just as Queen Elizabeth's best players would. When they play the old ballads, we recognise the words and join in, such a pleasant way to pass an evening and such good company. Amy laughs and claps with delight, her face flushed with pleasure and wine.

Then Owain and another Welshman called Rhoddri together tell the stories of the Mabinogi, of Rhiannon on her white horse always evading the knights who pursue her, as if by magic always able to keep three paces ahead, no matter how fast or how slowly their horses go. But we're shocked when we hear how she was falsely accused of murdering her child. The story has a happy ending when she's proved innocent of any crime. Amy's brown eyes grow large with wonder and fill with tears at Rhiannon's plight. Then we hear the story of the evil Blodeuwedd turned into an owl and condemned to live in darkness, shunned by the other birds, for her wickedness in plotting the hideous torture of the ruler, Lleu Llaw Gyffes.

The whole evening ends with the song 'Good Company' written by King Henry so many years ago. It's hard to let go after such a wonderful treat and reluctantly we say good night to the players who are shown to their sleeping quarters with the servants while Sir Anthony escorts Amy and Mrs Picto across the snow in the courtyard to the door of the staircase leading to the best chamber in the manor house. We hear Amy giggling as the wind causes the flame on her candle to flicker and go out. My small chamber in the southern wing of the house is just a short walk from Amy's and close to those of the other gentlewomen. As I undress I can hear the men servants and the musicians, under the effect of the ale they have drunk, talking a little too loudly in the rooms below as they make their way to bed. Soon their conversation and laughter will die down and the only sound will be that of the wind swirling the snowflakes round the sleeping house.

The visitors have to travel back to their farms and cottages the next day but not before Amy and I have time to settle a score with them! The five young men have said that they cannot imagine that two young ladies would be able to beat them at skittles so Amy has challenged them to a contest before they go home! Two teams are planned with Amy, Sir Anthony, Owain and me on one side and the other four young men on the other. I haven't seen Amy laugh so much for a long time as she does at the prospect of the match.

From my tiny window I watch Sir Anthony's lantern across the court yard, illuminating the door and the double flight of stairs leading to Amy's chamber. He pauses at the foot of the stairs to allow Amy to relight her candle from the lantern and then she mounts the first flight, turning on the landing to wave to him before ascending the short second flight of steps. We're all well fed, happy and slightly inebriated with the wine so it's a pity that I cannot laugh and chat with Amy as we once did, sitting on her bed until late at night. Although her chamber is the largest at Cumnor it's still not large enough for

191

me to have a bed in there – and Amy's bed is not large enough for me to share as we did when we were girls.

I watch Sir Anthony's lantern moving back past the Great Hall which is next to Amy's chamber. On the other side of her door lies the garden accessible through the little archway and I have no doubt that, in the morning, we will see the tiny paw prints of night visitors sniffing out any left over scraps outside the kitchen door.

While I settle down in my bed on the upper floor, I can still hear the men talking and the sounds of the women busying themselves in the kitchen and the buttery downstairs before they too retire to their own sleeping quarters. I hear Rhoddri's voice saying something in his strong Welsh accent and everyone laughs.

The following morning I'm awakened by a strange sound. It's barely light and very, very cold; shivering I pull my cloak around my shift and put on my sleeping bonnet which has fallen off during the night. Through the window, illuminated in the dazzling white of the newly fallen snow, I can see the male servants accompanied by Sir Anthony and the five musicians all shovelling snow which has drifted from the north into the south western corner of the court yard totally obscuring Amy's door and the doors to the Great Hall. The archway to the garden is lost in a wall of snow. It occurs to me that the road from Cumnor village, which is on the northern side of the Place will not be passable for some time. We are completely cut off.

Chapter Twenty Six
Owain

There is no game of skittles in the Long Gallery! All the men are required to clear the snow in the courtyard and to make a path through to the sheds and buildings where the animals and horses are kept. The milk in the dairy is frozen in the pail and the serving girls hasten to light the fires in the fireplaces around Cumnor Place. One of the young boys brings in logs and piles them up by the hearths. My bedchamber does not have a fireplace but Amy's has a warm fire and, of course, we're always welcome in the warmth of the kitchen with the glowing embers of its bread oven and the roasting spit over a hearty fire. The Long Gallery and Great Hall take a lot longer to warm through.

Before dark in the afternoon we all assemble in the Hall and Sir Anthony thanks everyone for their hard work. The animals are all bedded down for the night, he says, and well supplied with hay and we can now proceed around the Place thanks to the hard work of the men who have all helped to dig pathways through the snow. In recognition for such an effort, we will all eat together this evening in the Hall, ladies, gentlemen and servants.

So the long table is set for twenty four people. Once again there's a lavish supply of food, rabbit in a stew, roasted beef and liver, venison and tongue in pies and jellied brawn, tasty bread and pottage of beans and peas, preserved and dried in the summer.

After the first courses we have sweet tarts and pastries filled with preserves. There's no attempt to ration the food so we can only assume that there's enough at Cumnor, thanks to Sir Anthony's careful planning, to last all winter.

After the meal the servants clear the table and we all settle down again for another evening's entertainment by our players. While the servants busy themselves we talk, shyly at first, to the young musicians.

"Will your families not be anxious to know where you are?" asks Amy.

"Oh no," says Rhoddri, "This has happened before you know. They will manage at home without us and be grateful for the extra money we bring home." He winks. "Sir Anthony has promised to pay us well for each evening we are delayed here. You must be a very important lady."

John frowns at him. "You great fool, Rhoddri! Don't you know who this lady is?"

It's clear from the expression on Rhoddri's face that he does not.

"She's the wife of the most important man at court, idiot. This is Lady Dudley, wife of Sir Robert Dudley."

"So why are you not at court then?" Rhoddri blunders on in his sing song voice. "Had a row with your husband, have you?" He smiles and winks at John. "This lad here is always having rows with his wife."

There's a silence that's almost audible.

"What?" says Rhoddri, unabashed, "What did I say then."

"Are you married, Rhoddri," I ask, realising that this sounds a little forward but trying to rescue the situation none the less.

"No, not I," says Rhoddri with great emphasis, "And never will be either. My mother and father are glad when I come out with the players. Glad to get rid of me, you see!"

"And you Owain?" I ask.

Now it's my turn to be embarrassed, so much so that I want the ground to swallow me up. After another silence, John says quietly, "Owain lost his wife last summer, of the sweating sickness. He has two small children to look after."

My face is red with shame. "I'm so sorry, so very sorry. How stupid of me to pry so. Now I've spoiled everything."

Owain catches my sleeve as I get up to leave the Hall. "No, don't leave, Mistress Kat. It's not your fault. You were trying to be helpful. And don't worry for me as I'm learning to manage and I have very good kin who help me with the farm and the children. They're glad for me to be here at Cumnor for they know that a young man has to have an interest outside his work and his family and they know I love my music and story telling."

A tear rolls down my cheek as I feel my humiliation is complete; he's so kind hearted and the fact that he uses the familiar form of address to me makes me appreciate his kindness even more.

"Well then," says the irrepressible Rhoddri, "Skittles tomorrow then. But first ..... time for a jig." He jumps up and begins a lively tune. Owain picks up the drum to accompany him and the others caper around, acting the fool.

"And now," says Owain, "If we are all assembled again, we will have the story of the Lady of the Fountain."

195

The servants gather at the back of the hall and Sir Anthony's company of ladies seat themselves by the fireside as Owain begins his strange tale.

The snow stays for almost a week and, by the end of this time, we have a merry company of friends. Amy and I have not enjoyed ourselves so much for many years but all good things must come to an end. We awake one morning to the sound of dripping water; the weather has warmed a little, the snow has thawed and our musicians have to take the road out of Cumnor Place while they can. We go with them to the roadside and sadly wave goodbye.

"Do you think that we'll see them again in the summer," I ask, cautiously, a week later. I don't want Amy to realise my warm feelings for Owain and tease me.

I need not have worried. Amy's thoughts are with Robert again.

"Maybe, Kat, but first we have Easter and I'm quite sure that Robert will visit me again as he did last year and then I'll go to London with him and live at Christchurch House while he attends court. Of course I cannot go with him on the Queen's progress, no wife can go, but it may not be long before we find a manor house in Warwickshire and, when we do, I know that Robert will want to spend more time there with me." Amy chatters on.

My poor innocent friend! She hasn't heard the latest gossip about the goings on at court. Sir Anthony has forbidden all talk about Robert and Elizabeth in front of Amy and has said that he will dismiss any servant who does so. But this doesn't mean that they cannot talk when I'm there and the talk is shocking. Rumours abound even to the extent that the Queen is pregnant with Sir Robert's child, a shocking calumny, and it's difficult to separate truth from fantasy.

Robert sends his wife some embroidered slippers but Easter comes and goes and still there's no sign of him at Cumnor.

Chapter Twenty Seven
Humours of the Spleen

As a wet and cold spring passes into summer, there's still no longed-for reunion between Amy and her husband. He seems to have forgotten her very existence and Amy's mood becomes darker and darker.

Sir Anthony loves gardening and tries to interest Amy in the tiny young plants he is settling in the ground of the terraced garden but she's in a world of her own. We begin to worry about her health again as she loses weight and looks frail so Sir Anthony decides to send Bowes to Sir Robert in the hope that he, Robert, will take pity on his wife and pay her a visit. Unfortunately Sir Robert is obviously too busy with the Queen and sends his representative in the unwelcome personage of Thomas Blount, who is accompanied by his ruffian followers.

Blount offers a solution. "Sir Anthony, I am of the belief that Lady Dudley is melancholy and suffering from humours of the spleen. However I know of a certain doctor in the city of Oxford who has the best reputation in all England when it comes to dealing with such cases. Perhaps it would be wise if I were to ask this man for potions and powders to help my Lady …. before she wastes away and succumbs to death." He adds the last part when he sees Sir Anthony hesitate. No gentleman, Blount knows, will want to have the wife of a famous person die in his household.

Sir Anthony is completely taken in. "Yes, cousin Blount, this is a very good course of action. We must do all we can to effect a cure for the poor lady."

To my horror Blount gives a smile of satisfaction and sets out with his men for Oxford. The following day he returns in a vile mood.

I am not the only one to suspect a plot. The good doctor has not felt it wise to entrust any powders to Blount and his men. He has heard the gossip and realises that he's being set up to take the blame if Lady Dudley is poisoned. I breathe a sigh of relief and attempt to find other ways to lift Amy's black moods. Maybe I can reawaken her interest in fine clothes again.

I mention my plan to Sir Anthony and he says that he will write to Sir Robert and ask him to send some small gifts for his ailing wife. Surprisingly Robert responds with generosity sending several pairs of embroidered slippers and some new hoods. Amy's spirits lift when she thinks that her husband still cares for her. But her mood sinks again and the black dog of depression returns when she hears that the Queen has sent William Cecil from court to manage the situation at Leith in Scotland where the French are holding the fortress and where the English and Protestant Scottish lords have suffered a humiliating defeat. Without Cecil to caution Elizabeth about her relationship with Robert, the Queen is free to do as she wishes.

There's a rumour that Cecil is at the end of his tether over the scandal at court and may resign. He's finding it impossible to help the Queen to govern while her attention is completely taken up by her romantic attachment to Amy's husband. Sir Robert Dudley is so hated by the aristocracy that a civil war is feared if the Queen continues to favour him and the talk is now all about Robert divorcing his wife so that he and Elizabeth can be married.

Even Robert's greatest opponent has been dealt with by the Queen - the Duke of Norfolk was effectively 'banished' by being sent to command the garrison at Berwick in Northumberland when it was first feared that the French de Guise family, Mary Stuart's in laws, would try to invade England via Scotland. Mary sees herself as the rightful Queen of England as well as of France and Scotland but Elizabeth, while seething over this, can think of nothing and no one but Robert.

Blount and his men are back at Cumnor in late summer and are now trying another tactic – one that they have used before. They wait until Sir Anthony is not with Amy and then pretend to be taking a casual walk wherever Amy is located. Within earshot they discuss Robert's relationship with Elizabeth in small tantalising snatches. Elizabeth is on her summer progress again with Robert by her side, behaving as if he is her prince consort and without the disapproving presence of Cecil, so there is plenty of rumour and scandal to report.

"My Lord Robert is sending to Spain for some very fast horses," says Blount.

"Oh, and why is this?" says his man, feigning ignorance.

"So that the Queen can ride even faster when she's out hunting. She's a wonder, they say, and only my Lord Robert can keep up with her."

"Well that must be very convenient for them, everyone being left behind and the two of them heaven knows where …. all alone and deep in the forest like the stag and the doe. No wonder they want faster horses!"

Much sniggering and male laughter from Blount's men follows this. Amy's face is a picture of pain as she turns away from her tormentors.

But there's no escape. Like it or not Amy and I are going to be treated to a running account of her husband's unfaithfulness. And there's not a thing we can do about it.

I see another problem too. Amy's chamber at Cumnor Place is separated from all the others. It was given to her by Sir Anthony with the best of intentions because it's so much larger than any other but I fear for her now in her isolated state with only Mrs Picto for company each night. Were either of them to call out it's doubtful that anyone would hear.

By mid August Amy's mood changes again and she's suddenly very happy but won't say why. She writes a letter to her tailor, Mr Edney, in London requesting that he alter one of her favourite gowns so that the neckline will be as pretty as the one on the gown he made for her previously. This is indeed progress! I'm so happy that her spirits have lifted once more. And the fair at Abingdon is only a short while off so we have something to look forward to.

Later in the month Amy becomes very secretive and seems to be avoiding my presence for some reason. I see her sitting on the bench in the garden, looking out over the terraces and apparently enjoying the sweet scents of lavender and roses but her eyes are vacant and empty. When she sees me approach, she jumps up and walks off elsewhere, back to the seclusion of her chamber shutting the door firmly behind her, or into the churchyard and towards the church, or across the courtyard to our own little chapel where Mrs Picto says she often finds her praying, hands clasped, eyes tightly closed and on her knees. Something is going on; something that Amy has no wish to share with anyone.

Eventually September arrives and with it the day of Abingdon fair. Everyone in Cumnor Place has been looking forward to this for weeks. Everyone that is except Mrs Owen who says that Sunday is no day for a fair and that she will go the following day instead! Mrs Odingsells says that she will stay at Cumnor to keep the older lady company but that they will not spoil the day for the servants who are free to go. And Amy? No one knows what Amy wishes to do but the fair is such a rare treat that we all assume she will go with the rest of us.

What a surprise lies in store as we sit that morning in the Great Hall, eating breakfast and anticipating the pleasures of the day ahead.

Chapter Twenty Eight
Abingdon Fair

Everyone's scurrying round. The servants are clearing away the dishes from the table as fast as they can because no one wishes to waste a minute of this delightful holiday. There's no time to lose and the weather promises a lovely sunny day. Mr Bowes goes to help the men with the horses. But where's Amy?

My friend walks into the Hall and looks around with astonishment at all the clamour and excitement.

"Come quickly Lady Dudley. The carriage will be here soon and you need to eat some cold meat and bread before the journey," says one of the serving girls.

"Carriage? Journey?" says Amy.

"Don't worry, Amy," I offer an explanation although I cannot for the life of me think how Amy could have forgotten the fair. "We're not going on another long journey. She means the carriage to take us to the fair in Abingdon. Had you forgotten?"

"Fair? Abingdon?" Amy seems in a trance and her thoughts are a world away.

"Yes indeed it will be a wonderful treat. Think of all the ribbons we can buy and the musicians and jugglers. All the nice food to buy too! We may see our friends from Christmas again – you remember? Owain and his troupe may be there with their merry tales and romances."

"I'm not going. I don't want to go."

"Of course you do! You said some weeks ago, when you sent your dress away to be altered, that you would wear it to the Abingdon fair."

"Didn't you hear me?" Amy's voice rises to screaming pitch. "I said I'm not going and I mean I – am – not – going!"

The clamour in the Hall has stopped now as all eyes are on Amy.

"Are you expecting a visitor my lady?" asks one of the servants trying to be helpful.

"No I am NOT!" screams Amy which makes me wonder if she is.

"Shall I stay and keep you company?" I venture warily.

"You most certainly will not," shouts Amy. "It's none of your business what I choose to do. Go," she glares round at the astonished company of servants and gentlewomen, "Go away, all of you and LEAVE ME ALONE."

After a shocked silence, Mrs Odingsells says, "Well I for one will not be going away, Lady Dudley. I intend to stay here with Mrs Owen. So you will have at least two other people to keep you company and that is an end to the matter." She draws herself up to her full height and stalks away. Amy runs after her and a fearsome argument develops.

"Amy …" I begin, softly holding out my hand in friendship and trying to pull her to one side. This is so unseemly and the servants are gawping, open mouthed.

"Oh go away, Kat," she says in a tiny tired voice after all her shouting. She snatches her hand from mine. "I want to be left on my own."

With this Amy turns on her heel and walks out of the Great Hall across the courtyard and up to her bedchamber, slamming and bolting the door behind her.

"Come, Mistress Katherine," says Sir Anthony, who has just walked in to witness Amy's outburst of temper, "There is nothing you can do when someone is in such a mood except to leave them to their own ill humour. But it is most unlike Lady Dudley, I have to remark. Maybe we will find her changed when we return and I fear that any further attempts at persuasion will only make her more passionate. Come and enjoy the fair with everyone else."

The servants have recovered from their embarrassment at Amy's behaviour and I guess that Sir Anthony is quite right and that we will find Amy's mood has lightened by the time we return. I'll buy her something pretty to cheer her and perhaps she'll go to the fair tomorrow with Mrs Owen and Mrs Odingsells. The carriage is brought and Sir Anthony's wife, Mrs Picto and I get inside. Mr Bowes is mounted on his own horse as is Sir Anthony, who has allowed the servants to share rides on our two other horses and a mule. The rest walk on foot until it is their turn to ride.

So our little procession winds its way down the hillside and turns south towards Abingdon. The servants laugh and sing as we go along, Sir Anthony smiles benignly at his little family anticipating the fun of the day ahead just as so many small children would do.

At the fair there's a lot to see and, if you have enough money, to buy. Fruit tartlets and spiced hams, eggs and cheeses, sweet meats and fresh fruit, spices and herbs all displayed in a tempting fashion. Sir Anthony lingers over the plants, asking questions – how will this bush stand up when the Cumnor wind blows strong and what colour will the flowers be on

205

this one and will it attract the bees and provide good honey. He is in his own private paradise.

There are acrobats too, jugglers and trained animals, hawks and dogs and, sad to see, a poor old bear that is forced to dance by vicious prods from a cane in its handler's fist. The man with the bear looks like a gypsy and is surrounded by some equally dark and swarthy companions and I make up my mind to keep my distance.

There are pretty things to buy, ribbons and pomanders, caps, bonnets and slippers. And then there are the musicians and the men performing stories and masques, fascinating to watch. We buy cherries from the baskets of the fruit sellers and stand to enjoy each performance.

Suddenly, while I am enthralled by an enactment of the adventures of Guy of Warwick, I feel a light touch on my shoulder. It is none other than Owain, the farmer, musician and story teller for whom I'd felt such sympathy the previous Christmas when I'd heard of the death of his wife.

"Well, Mistress Katherine, I do believe; and how have you been faring this long time since we last met?"

I blush deeply and manage to stammer an incoherent reply. Owain is even more handsome than I remember.

He smiles and asks where Lady Dudley is and when I reply that I am here without the pleasant company of my dear friend, Owain offers his arm and suggests that we explore the fair together. He is all smiles and courtesy as he ignores the amiable jibes and teasing of his friends who grin annoyingly as they watch me take his arm. When we reach the place where Sir Anthony is still pondering which plants to take home, the good gentleman gives me an old fashioned look and raises his eyebrows in such a way that I can't help laughing. I'm so happy and comfortable in Owain's company that I completely forget my poor friend in her lonely and miserable state at Cumnor Place.

All too soon the afternoon draws to a close and I suddenly remember that I'd promised myself that I would buy a present for Amy. But what to buy? There's so much to choose from.

"I know the very thing," says Owain and leads me to a table where an old woman is selling pomanders. Here we choose an orange stuck all over with cloves except for a cross where a velvet ribbon encircles it, like an orb carried by a queen. The smell of the citrus and the cloves is divine and I know that Amy will love such a treasure.

"It will protect her from disease too," says Owain with a hint of practicality that makes me laugh.

I board the carriage again with the gentlewomen and my gallant Welsh story teller helps me up and promises to come to see me at Cumnor before very long. And at this stage I have no idea just how quickly his promise will be realised.

As we travel home we're a very merry company. When we reach the hill leading to Cumnor Place, I get out of the carriage to give our poor horse an easier task and walk along with the servants laughing and singing.

"Oh dear, Mistress Katherine," says Sir Anthony jokingly as he rides past us, "You will never make a fine lady of the court."

No, I think, and I never want to be. I want to be the wife of a farmer, a farmer called Owain!

We trundle slowly past the churchyard and into the courtyard at Cumnor where Mr Bowes and the servants take the sweating horses round to the trough for a well earned drink and then to the stable yard to enable them to cool off before they're turned out onto the field. The boys take old rags to rub them down so they will not get a chill in the cool air of evening.

The serving girls and I go to the Great Hall to see whether Amy, Mrs Owen and Mrs Odingsells have enjoyed the cold meats the girls left out for them but finding the two older ladies playing cards and no sign of my friend, I make my way with Mrs Picto to the door leading to Amy's chamber. But I begin to have a strange feeling; why was Amy not in the Great Hall with the other two? They said they had not seen her all afternoon and assumed she was taking a rest upstairs.

As we walk across the now empty courtyard I have a sense of impending doom, an uneasy feeling that lies in the pit of my stomach. Mrs Picto, ahead of me, reaches the door leading to the stairs that go up to Amy's chamber, opens it and gives a piercing scream.

Over her shoulder I see my dearest friend lying at the bottom of the steps, her head twisted in an unnatural way. Even before I rush over to her and fall down on my knees to take her hand, I know that she's dead.

Chapter Twenty Nine
Scandal

Mrs Picto's scream brings everyone running. Sir Anthony pushes his way through the group of servants crowding the door.

"What is it? What has happened?"

"It's Lady Dudley, Sir," says Mrs Picto, wailing, "She must have fallen down the stairs."

"Is she breathing?" Sir Anthony bends over the body and holds his hand to her throat.

"No, Sir," I reply, "She's quite cold. She must have been lying here for some time." My voice is hushed and I can hardly speak the words. I feel as if I am about to choke.

Mrs Odingsells is at the back of the assembled group now and is followed by Mrs Owen who walks slowly with a cane for assistance. "Has Lady Dudley had an accident?"

"Yes," says Sir Anthony, "It appears that she has fallen down the stairs and broken her neck." He lifts Amy's head from its unnatural position and lays it straight. I can see that there is no stiffness; the head is as floppy as that on a rag doll and yet the fall has not dislodged the little lace cap that she wears around the manor house when she is not receiving visitors or dressing for dinner. On other, more formal occasions she would be wearing her finery and decorated hoods.

"Did you not hear anything?" Sir Anthony asks Mrs Odingsells. No use asking Mrs Owen who is as deaf as a post.

"Well I did think I heard a sound as we were playing cards early in the afternoon. It was as if someone had dropped something but we knew we were alone in the house and I believed that the cat had been after the cream in the buttery again and had knocked over the jug."

"It was quite a clatter. Even *I* heard it. I thought the wind had blown a bench over in the courtyard," said Mrs Owen. "We laughed about it, didn't we Mrs Odingsells?"

The full implication of what has happened is now beginning to reach me and I can see from Sir Anthony's worried frown that the same thought is occurring to him. The wife of one of England's foremost courtiers has been found dead in his house and under circumstances that are not at all clear. It is entirely possible that Amy could have taken her own life because of her agitated state of mind just before we departed. Heaven knows that her husband had given her cause for such agitation.

But the whole affair will reflect badly upon Sir Anthony and his household. Perhaps he should not have left her in an empty house with only two elderly ladies for company. Perhaps people will think that she was not cared for adequately at Cumnor Place. Worse still, in view of all the gossip surrounding Sir Robert Dudley and the Queen, people may suspect foul play.

"We will have to send for the coroner," says Sir Anthony, "And Sir Robert will have to be informed as quickly as possible, naturally." He looks at the darkening sky. "Unfortunately it is now too late to do anything of practical value."

Sir Anthony summons Mr Bowes and two of the stable lads. "Help me to carry Lady Dudley up to her chamber. We will lay her down on the bed until we can start the necessary proceedings tomorrow. Mrs

Picto and Mistress Katherine please follow us. Perhaps you will keep a night vigil over Lady Dudley's body."

Mrs Picto and I light the candles in Amy's chamber and take up our seats either side of the body in the two chairs that Sir Anthony brings up for us. We take it in turn to go down to the Great Hall to eat but we have little appetite. Stiff and uncomfortable we watch over Amy, Lady Dudley, as she begins her final sleep of all and we're glad when the first rays of light shine through the shutters in the morning.

Everything then happens very quickly. Mr Bowes saddles his horse and prepares to ride to Windsor where it is believed he will find Sir Robert, given that the court is already there. The coroner and an undertaker are sent for and arrive with a horse drawn cart and a bier on which Amy's body is placed. There will need to be an inquest to ascertain the cause of death so we have not laid out the body, washing it and placing it in a shroud, as would be normal. The undertaker's women will perform that final ritual after the members of the coroner's court have carried out their inspection. I know what the procedure will be – my friend's naked body will be placed before the court so that the men can pull it this way and that to search for any marks that may provide clues. How Amy would have hated to think that she would suffer such an undignified end.

As they depart, a group of the cottagers at Cumnor has already assembled outside on the road to pay their respects. News will spread fast and I wonder what the local people will make of it. We make our way back to the house and wait for events to unfold.

Cumnor Place today is a very different household to the one that awoke to the prospect of a fair and a holiday. The servants speak in whispers and the two older gentlewomen keep to their own chambers. Country folk are very superstitious and the day after Amy's body was discovered they're already claiming to have seen certain signs, a mist over the pond out of which a lone swan took flight, a flock of ravens in the meadow, the shepherd's dog that sits each night on the terrace by Amy's door and now howls continually at the sky and a dove that is trying to enter Amy's shuttered window instead of the dove cote.

The following day one of the servants returns from Cumnor village and says that all the talk is of how Sir Robert will be free to marry the Queen now that his wife has been murdered. Sir Anthony is distraught; his reputation it seems is in ruins but his mind is put at ease by the arrival of someone that Amy would not have been pleased to see had she still been alive. By midday Blount stands in the courtyard.

"Welcome Cousin Blount," says Sir Anthony, ushering the new arrival into the hall, "We had not expected to see someone from court so quickly."

"No indeed," says Blount, "And I would have been here even sooner had I not stopped overnight at the inn at Abingdon to ascertain what the folk there made of this sad matter."

"But Mr Bowes only set off with the news yesterday morning. Surely he did not reach Windsor in time for you to set off, stay overnight in Abingdon and arrive by this morning. That would have been a ride for him of merely a few hours and from here to

Windsor it's a distance of almost forty miles. Where did he find such fast horses?"

Blount smiles his lop sided smile. "By strange coincidence, I was already travelling north to Cumnor yesterday when I met Mr Bowes changing horses at the post inn at Wallingford. He told me of Lady Dudley's death and the strange circumstances surrounding it. So I decided to stay the night at Abingdon to hear what the local gossips had to say. After all," he leans back in his chair, "My Lord Robert will not be pleased if suspicion falls on him."

"Why should it? Lady Dudley had a fall down the stairs that is all. There is no hint of foul play; it was merely an accident."

"Put your mind at ease," says Blount easily, "There is no reason to think of blame in the matter, either for your good self or for my Lord. The people in the tavern at Abingdon had nothing but praise for you and said it was plainly bad fortune that this had happened at the home of someone they respected as an honest and kind man."

Sir Anthony is calmed by these words but not entirely at ease. There will be a long road before the matter is settled.

In the days that follow letters fly to and from Windsor. We hear that Sir Robert was shocked to the core by Amy's death and has retreated alone to his house at Kew where he dresses in black mourning clothes and avoids company. Is this the action of a murderer? Or, more probably, could it be the action of a hypocrite?

Blount is still with us and has tried to supervise the choice of a jury for the coroner but he is too late; the jury has been appointed already. According to

Cousin Blount, Sir Robert, in an attempt to distance himself from any accusation of influencing the verdict, had asked for them all to be strangers to him but well respected men who will make wise judgements without indulging in idle chatter.

At the end of the week I have a surprise visitor. It's Owain, come to express his sorrow for me at the loss of my friend.

"Owain! What an unexpected pleasure this is."

"Dear Mistress Katherine I'm delighted to see you again and would have been here sooner but," he looks around to see if anyone is close by and whispers, "I wished to see if I could bring any comfort over the matter of Lady Dudley's death."

I drop my voice though I don't see that there's any reason to, "What comfort could there be? I've lost a dear friend."

Owain pauses, as if he does not know where to begin, then says, "You do realise that the jury was considering that she may have taken her own life."

"Oh no, sweet Jesus! She would never do such a thing. Amy prayed every day; she would not commit such a vile act. Besides she had just sent a dress to her tailor for alteration. You do not know Amy as I do. She knew that she was very pretty and wanted to look her best at all times. Is that the act of someone who's plotting to murder herself?"

"Katherine, keep calm. You're right of course and you, of all people, knew her best but you cannot blame the jury for considering such a disgraceful act since many have said that she was in a strange mood that day and wanted to be left completely alone."

"But even if, and I say 'if', she'd planned such a thing, surely she would not have thrown herself down such a small flight of steps. She would have fallen forwards and put her hands out by compulsion, I think, to save herself. No, there would be other, more certain, ways to take her own life. Oh yes, and don't forget that Amy had always feared that she would be poisoned and was most careful not to let that happen. No, no, it's impossible. She must have tripped and fallen violently. Maybe she had had too much wine at midday and was not mindful of the steps and her skirts."

"Well I'm truly sorry, Katherine, to have caused you such distress by speaking carelessly and out of turn. I believed that you would have had such thoughts yourself and I only wanted to reassure you that the jury has now ruled out a verdict of suicide, one of the reasons being that they do not wish to bring such shame on Lady Dudley or, indeed, on her husband. This means that she will now be able to have a normal Christian burial when her body is released."

Of course Owain's quite right and this should be a great comfort to me. The murder of oneself is as bad as the murder of any other person and some think it's worse as the perpetrator can never confess and make peace with God and is therefore sentenced to eternal damnation. This is why I'm convinced that Amy would not place her soul in danger. Anyway Owain's news means we can now be sure that her funeral will go ahead with the dignity she deserves.

"How do you know what the jury is pondering anyway," I ask.

"Hush," says Owain, "Keep your voice down. You remember John who took part in our entertainment last Christmas?" I do.

215

"Well," continues my friend, "He's a man of considerable wealth and is highly respected. He only plays in our little troupe as a pastime because he owns a large farm to the south of Oxford – much bigger than my small holding," he adds modestly. "And he's a member of the jury. That's how I know."

Chapter Thirty
After The Funeral

As Owain said, Amy's body was released for burial some days later and she was laid to rest in the Church of Mary the Virgin in Oxford.

Back at Cumnor Place, Mrs Picto and I have sorted through Amy's precious possessions and sent them on their way to the people who would like to have them, the most expensive jewels have gone to Sir Robert Dudley (and are possibly destined for the Queen) while the gowns and hoods, slippers and sentimental reminders have gone back to her own kin in Norfolk and Camberwell. The strange note that I found in her sewing apron is now under the floorboard in Amy's chamber, in the place where it will remain forever or, at least, until someone finds it when we are long dead and gone.

But the note is never far from my thoughts. Why did I tell no one? I think that I'm just too scared of the consequences. Was she really expecting to see Robert round about the time of the fair and was that why she was so agitated and anxious to be alone? If I told anyone and if Amy's death was not a natural one, it would be all too easy for the murderer to return here, destroy the note and dispatch me at the same time. Hence I trust no one with the knowledge.

The jury has still not released its findings. Presumably, having ruled out suicide, they're not satisfied that Amy's death was an accident either. Nor am I. But who would have wanted such a thing? What would anyone have to gain?

The obvious answer would be that Robert and the Queen could marry but Robert's behaviour suggests that he sees this as a personal tragedy regarding his ambitions in that direction. He can hardly marry the Queen if he is suspected of the murder of his wife.

Elizabeth too has attempted to demonstrate her shock and sorrow at Amy's death by ordering that the whole court go into mourning for a month. But people are not fooled and think that this is the depths of hypocrisy. Amy's death had been eagerly anticipated by her not so long ago! Will this 'mourning' dissipate the rumours? I doubt it.

The gossip is, of course, that Robert had 'arranged' for his wife to be murdered. But even if his men had carried out such a deed without his knowledge surely they would have realised that such a clumsy attempt would cast doubts over the manner of her death and would have implicated 'Milord Robert'. They would have been providing him with no favours.

That only leaves one possibility. Had someone at court had Amy murdered, someone so ruthless that they would dispatch an innocent woman knowing that the scandal would ruin the possibility that the Queen could ever marry her favourite? But then, if that were the case, why even go to the trouble to make the death look like an accident by arranging the body at the foot of the stairs. If the jury decided that it was nothing more than a grave misfortune, such enemies of Robert would see their worst fears confirmed and he and the Queen would be free to marry.

No, no, Amy's death has to be an accident albeit a strange one. As I am turning these thoughts round and round in my mind, Sir Anthony comes in.

"Katherine I have some good news for you! I have found you a position as a gentlewoman

218

companion to Mrs Odingsells when she leaves Cumnor in a few days time."

Good news! It is the worst possible news - to be bound to this somewhat grumpy older lady for the rest of my days. I had hoped to stay at Cumnor where I might at least be able to see Owain from time to time. In my confusion I can only think of one thing to say.

"Thank you, Sir Anthony. It's kind of you to think of me and what of Mrs Picto? Is she to come with us?"

"No indeed, Mrs Owen has already asked for Mrs Picto be help her in her old age. Picto will dress her and attend to her needs."

Poor Picto! but I expect it's better than being turned out to beg for one's living. Sir Anthony must be able to read the disappointment on my face. "My dear Katherine," he says, "I hope to buy Cumnor Place but I am by no means sure as yet that this will happen and even if it does I will bring all my own servants here and my wife has her own group of gentlewomen. I'm afraid that there will be no room for other people. And Mrs Odingsells is a good woman. She will provide for your needs in the way to which you are accustomed. If you are happy with this arrangement you will leave tomorrow."

"Yes indeed, Sir Anthony, and I am very fortunate and do indeed thank you for your concern."

Sir Anthony smiles and bows out of the hall, leaving me once more to my thoughts. Tomorrow! No time to say farewell to dear Owain and no time to write a letter to him either for I must pack away my belongings.

The following morning we're up early and the grooms have the tiny carriage ready. Mrs Odingsells and I are helped in and I take a last look at Cumnor Place which I will never see again in all probability. The wheels bump and rumble down the road. We're heading for Berkshire where Mrs Odingsells and I will live with her son and his family and I'm empty and sick to my stomach.

I've never felt so alone in my whole life and can't help feeling that I should have been allowed at least to return to my lovely Norfolk, maybe to help Amy's half brother and his wife ...... or even to Hertfordshire, to the household of Mr Hyde. But who would want to take care of a spinster now approaching her twenty eighth birthday? What use am I to anyone? I'm not even pretty; not that being pretty helped dear Amy much. No, I'll live and die an old maid now.

Katherine! Stop feeling sorry for yourself! You're fortunate to have somewhere to live and you'll have to look on the brighter side. I force myself to stop being miserable and make as pleasant conversation as I can muster to Mrs Odingsells.

The morning is almost over and we're thinking about stopping for some refreshment, not that I'm hungry. Sir Anthony's groom is driving the litter and he feels that the horse needs a rest and some water so we stop outside an inn and prepare to alight. Behind us there's the sound of a horseman riding hard down the road and, turning round, we can see he's hidden in a cloud of dust.

"*He*'s in a hurry!" says Mrs Odingsells.

He pulls his sweating horse to a halt a few yards from us and leaps to the ground, his face grimy with dirt and sweat. We instinctively step backwards as he strides towards us. Thoughts are tumbling through my brain …. Amy, her broken neck, the note, Robert's men, run, run, run …. but I'm rooted to the spot. So this is it then, this is how it all ends, on a road outside a country tavern in broad daylight.

But, as he comes closer, I'm taken aback to see Owain and even more astonished when he says, "Mistress Katherine, do not leave me. Marry me, please do."

Chapter Thirty One
Knight in Shining Armour!

We must look a pretty sight! Mrs Odingsells, Sir Anthony's groom and I are all staring at Owain with our mouths wide open.

After what seems like an age Mrs Odingsells bursts out laughing, "Well what are you waiting for, Mistress Katherine? Say 'Yes'! Unless you want to spend the rest of your life with an old woman like me," she adds with a grimace.

For some unknown reason I burst into floods of tears; relief, remorse for what I'd been thinking, Mrs Odingsells' unexpected kindness, the realisation of my greatest wish – all these things combine to reduce me to a gibbering, sobbing idiot. Surely Owain will not want me now!

"I'd been thinking to ask you since the fair but, what with all the sad events at Cumnor, I somehow did not. I liked you when I first met you last Christmas but I thought that you, as a gentlewoman who is used to so much better, would not want a life with a poor farmer with two children already. I didn't have the courage to ask you for I thought you would say no but when I got to Cumnor this morning and found that you had gone, I rode as fast as I could to be here. But I …. I ….. do understand if you do not wish …… to come back with me ….. I understand …." Now it's Owain who's gibbering!

"Say yes," urges Mrs Odingsells, "Before he changes his mind."

A small crowd from the inn, attracted by the sound of the galloping horse, has been gathering around our little group. "Say yes," they urge, "Say yes." Sir Anthony's groom is laughing so much that I think he will fall over. "This is just like one of his stories," he tells the crowd, "When the knight finds the princess."

With Owain's grimy face and dust covered clothes and my face red and swollen with crying, we hardly look like a prince and princess, but I pull myself together and try to muster some dignity.

"Yes," I say to the cheers of the onlookers.

Inside the inn the landlord opens his best wine and Owain is embarrassed because he has no money to pay for it. "I will pay as a gift," says the landlord but Mrs Odingsells insists that she will do so. I'm now so sorry for her.

"What will you do?" I ask. "You'll have no one to keep you company."

"Nonsense, my son will know of other gentlewomen, even though I will not enjoy their company as much as I have enjoyed yours, Kat." These kind words make me cry all over again. Mrs Odingsells now asks the landlord for a pen and a paper. She writes a note to Sir Anthony explaining that I am about to be married and asking if I can stay at Cumnor for another week until the wedding can be arranged.

So I am about to be made the happiest woman in the world and I wonder what the chances will now be for another couple - Elizabeth and her 'sweet Robin'.

Chapter Thirty Two
A Secret Wedding

It's Advent 1560. In a bedchamber at a Seymour residence in Cannon Row, London, another Katherine and her beloved 'Ned', the young Earl of Hertford, are about to be married in a secret ceremony. The two young people are passionately in love and determined that no one will prevent their wedding – not even Queen Elizabeth herself.

Ned produces a ring, five links beautifully inscribed with a poem he has composed for the occasion, and Katherine, who has always been led by her heart rather than her brain, gives a gasp of pleasure when she sees it. Ned grasps her hand and looks at her directly; he raises his eyebrows and gives her a secret, knowing smile, which makes her giggle as it always does. The priest coughs to draw their attention to the solemnity of the occasion, getting married is not a frivolous event and not to be entered into lightly.

Ned and Katherine become serious, the priest recites the marriage ceremony and, after they have made their vows, pronounces them man and wife. There is only one witness, Ned's younger sister named Jane Seymour after her royal ancestor. The couple thank the priest who allows himself a smile and a sigh. Ah, these impetuous youngsters, do they really know what they are entering into?

The four in the wedding party help themselves to some refreshments that have been left out for them, after which the priest leaves soon followed by Jane. Then the newly weds are left alone in the chamber

224

where they strip off their clothes as quickly as possible and jump into bed.

Do they really know what they're doing? Katherine is the younger sister of the executed Queen, Lady Jane Grey, who died with her husband Lord Guildford Dudley almost eight years ago. In the event of Queen Elizabeth's death she would have a claim to the throne of England to rival that of Mary, Queen of Scots – and some would say a better claim since Katherine is a Protestant and therefore more acceptable to the people than Mary. If Elizabeth puts a tiny foot out of line, Katherine could well become the centre of a conspiracy to overthrow the Queen.

Worse still, Ned is first cousin to the now deceased King Edward VI and has a not insubstantial claim to the English crown himself. Between them the couple eclipse all other members of the nobility in their suitability to rule the country and produce male heirs. Elizabeth had better watch out!

The storm clouds gather.

Chapter Thirty Three
September 1561 - One Year After Amy's Death

I can't tell you how much the life of a farmer's wife
suits me! Owain and I have been married now for
over a year and we have three children, his small boy
aged three named Henry, a little girl of two, Dwyfor,
who was still a newborn baby when her mother died,
and our own tiny baby, Llewellyn. The work is hard
but I learned how to cook and bake bread from the
servants at Mr Hyde's when Amy would eat nothing
that I had not prepared for her. And I can sew and
make clothes for the little ones.

Owain has help on the farm and we're doing
well. We have two farm hands and a girl who works
in the dairy and the kitchen and I'm helped with the
children by the parents of his first wife who live in a
cottage close by and treat me as if I were their own
daughter. They're happy to be close to their own
grandchildren and our little girl and boys will always
live in a world of love and happiness, far away from
the diseases and plagues of the court and royal
palaces.

Robert and Elizabeth have still not married. We
hear from Owain's contacts that Elizabeth sought to
make Robert an earl soon after Amy's death and this
was seen by many as an attempt to ennoble him so
there could be no objection to her marrying a
commoner. But William Cecil had pointed out that
Sir Robert now had so many enemies among the
nobility that such an act, and so soon after his wife's
death, would only lead to infighting and civil war.
Apparently Elizabeth had been filling out the
document making Robert 'Earl of Leicester' when

Cecil stopped her - so she took a dagger and slashed the document again and again in temper and frustration. Amy, were you looking down and laughing!

One evening Owain comes home with some startling news. The inquest into Amy's death has finally made public its findings – an accident says the jury - and did I know, he says, that Amy had suffered two head wounds from the fall!

No, I did not; and what is more I did not see how that could possibly be the case. Her cap had been still on her head when we found her and there were no blood stains there at all.

"How could Amy have suffered wounds to her head and not have bled profusely? Were they small wounds?" I ask.

Owain is amazed at what I say. Her cap must have been soaked in blood, he says. One of the wounds was the size of two thumbs in depth and the report calls them 'dints' which implies they were sustained in a violent way as might a soldier receive such a blow in battle.

"Perhaps she hit her head on a step."

"What – twice?"

"There were two wounds, you are sure of this?"

"There were indeed but the report still says that her death was an accident."

"What do you think, Owain?"

"I think it's suspicious, Kat. For there to have been a deep wound and no blood reported at the scene can only mean one thing. She must have suffered the dints somewhere else, in another chamber at Cumnor maybe; which would mean that her body was placed at the foot of the stairs to make it look like an accident, or to make it seem as if she had taken her own life."

I cast my mind back and wrack my brains to try to recall the scene. There was no puddle of blood, I'm sure of it.

"But who would have done such a thing?" I venture. Owain and I have often wondered about the circumstances of her death and the strange case of the note I found in the pocket of her sewing apron, a note which was not in Sir Robert's handwriting but purported to be from him.

"All the usual suspects can be eliminated, if you ask me," says Owain, "But there's something I have not yet told you, Kat; something which I thought strange at the time and which I later dismissed as having no significance."

"What – you mean that you saw Richard Verney at the fair? There's been so much gossip about that."

"No, I have no idea who that gentleman is and would not recognise him if I fell over him. I know that it was rumoured that he was at the fair but what motive would he have for killing Amy? Unless it was a bungled attempt to win Sir Robert's favour by doing something he'd not been asked to do."

"Well it's possible."

"There's another possibility you know. And you have to ask yourself who has the most to gain from Amy's death."

"I don't understand."

Owain hesitates as if he does not like to voice his suspicions. "Remember that I told you how I went to Spain as a young man to learn about the way they made tapestries and crafted fine metals for daggers, swords and drinking cups?"

228

I do. I love these stories of foreign lands that Owain tells the children at bedtime. He continues, "My travels took me to southern Spain to a place called Ronda and then to Seville. Eventually I met a group of Spanish noblemen who were travelling to England to be in the company of the ambassador at Mary's court."

"Ambassador de Feria?"

"Yes the Count de Feria. These young men needed a translator and by this time I could speak both Spanish and English as well as my native tongue, Welsh. So I came back to Mary's court with them at the time that Robert Dudley was striving to gain acceptance among Prince Philip's men. They were, of course, using him because they needed help to fight their battles – remember St Quentin and that ghastly business of Henry's death?"

I certainly do. Robert was not the same man after seeing his little brother torn to pieces by a cannon ball right in front him.

Owain goes on. "But Robert was ambitious and eager to get himself and his brothers back in Mary's favour after their humiliating disgrace over the Jane Grey affair."

"Yes, we know all this but what has it to do with Amy's death," I ask impatiently.

"Now remember the time when we were at the fair at Abingdon," says Owain. "I forgot all else when I met you again on that day but now I remember seeing some others that I knew. They didn't recognise me; I'm a poor farmer now and they last saw me wearing fine clothes at Mary's court. Do you remember the man with the dancing bear?"

"Yes the poor creature, I certainly do."

229

"He had with him two companions."

"Hm …. I don't remember."

"Well I can tell you that he did and perhaps the people of Abingdon thought that they were Welsh and speaking Welsh for they were dark haired and dark skinned as we are. But they were not from our country; they were Spaniards and I now recall some little snatches of conversation they were having."

"About Amy?"

"About something they had done; a deed completed, a duty performed. And they spoke about the Bishop. At the time I thought nothing of it."

"The Bishop?"

"De la Quadra, the new ambassador."

"I'm not following you. What had the Spanish to do with the fair at Abingdon? Surely you do not think ….. but why would the Spanish want Amy dead?"

"You have to think, Kat, who wins and who loses. Either Robert and the Queen marry after Amy's death and there is protest and civil war or they do not marry and the Queen is free to marry Archduke Charles, a Hapsburg cousin of King Philip of Spain. Either way the Spanish win and we all know that many would have welcomed any marriage rather than one to a Dudley."

"But I still don't understand. How would the Spaniards gain from a civil war in England?"

"You, of all people, Kat, remember the Jane Grey affair or should I say Queen Jane?"

"Yes, but …."

"Jane had a sister, your namesake, Katherine."

"Who was married at fourteen to Henry Lord Herbert and then divorced from him when her father

230

was declared a traitor. Amy and I were at their wedding and she was heartbroken about the divorce for she loved him dearly. And Henry loved her but he had to obey his father."

"So Katherine was then free to marry elsewhere and do you realise, Kat, that she has as great a claim to the throne as Mary, Queen of Scots. So if Elizabeth died childless – and some people claim she cannot have children even if she marries – or if there is a civil war and Elizabeth has to renounce her throne, then Katherine Grey would be the obvious choice for the people of England. Her claim would be better than that of Mary Queen of Scots - a Frenchwoman who is also a Catholic."

"But what has this to do with Amy's death?"

"Now does it surprise you if I tell you that the Spanish have long plotted to marry Katherine Grey to a Hapsburg nobleman? I know this from the time I spent at court translating for the Spanish."

At this point I remember with a shiver the garden one evening at Camberwell when Amy and I overheard Blount and Verney talking about Elizabeth's ill treatment of Jane Dormer.

Blount's words come floating back to me, "Well I expect Jane Dormer deserved it. Her husband can't stand Elizabeth, that's why he's quitting. He thinks her reign will end in tears and there'll be a rebellion against our good Lord Robert when the Queen marries him. Rumour has it that Feria's wife has been trying to smuggle Jane Grey's sister out of the country so she can marry a Spanish Hapsburg."

"What? Katherine Grey? Now there's a flighty little piece!" said Verney.

Blount laughed. "She certainly is. But, after Elizabeth, she has as good a claim to the throne as Mary Stuart. And what's more she's not a Scottish Frenchwoman like the Queen of Scots. If there's a rebellion against Elizabeth and Robert, the Spanish want to bring Katherine and her Hapsburg husband back."

"So who wins?" says Owain, bringing my thoughts back to the present. "I'll tell you who. If Elizabeth was deposed because of her refusal to give up Robert, the Spanish would have had Katherine Grey and her husband, a representative of their own, on the English throne just as they did in Philip and Mary's time."

"Do you think this will still happen, Owain?" I ask.

"Not likely! Katherine, the crafty little vixen, made a secret marriage with Ned, Lord Hertford, about last Christmas time!"

"What! Without the Queen's permission?"

"Exactly! And Elizabeth was furious, for it makes Katherine with her English nobleman husband a very suitable replacement for her should there be a plot to remove the Queen from the throne. It makes Elizabeth fear the assassin's dagger too. She won't give anyone an excuse for conspiring against her and this means she cannot now marry her Robert. It would be too dangerous. It also means that all the plotting of the Spanish was to no avail and Katherine is now taken off the marriage list for the Hapsburgs."

"It also means that, if Amy was murdered by the Spanish in a plot to vilify Robert and Elizabeth and make way for a Queen Katherine and her intended

Spanish husband, my dear sweet friend has died for no purpose. She could have lived after all."

"And now it seems that everyone has lost, despite all the scheming. Elizabeth will have to distance herself from all the scandal and this means keeping her distance from Robert. The best they can hope for from now on will be a friendship." Owain smiles a satisfied smile. Like so many he does not like Robert Dudley either.

"In the bear pit of court life, my lovely Kat, every one's a loser."

"We're so fortunate to have each other and all the love in the world, Owain." And after a while I add, "I wonder if they will still talk of this affair in the future or whether it will all be forgotten and I wonder, if they do, what they will think of it. Will anyone ever discover the truth behind Amy's death?"

Epilogue
Autumn 1588

I'm back at Stanfield Hall in Norfolk and sitting on a
low wall. The year is 1549. Amy is riding the new
horse that Robert has given her and which she's
called Pavane. Amy's hat falls off as she canters
circles around Robert who is regarding her with some
concern as Pavane goes faster and faster.

"Oi con't stop'ur," says Amy laughing and in her
broad Norfolk accent.

"Sit up straight. I've told you before, Amy, if
you lean forward she'll go faster. She's trained to do
that."

"Now Oi lost moi stirrup," yells Amy, her golden
curls flying out behind her.

Robert rushes forward in concern and grabs the
bridle bringing the horse to a dead stop. Amy lurches
forward like a cloth doll and Robert catches her as she
leaves the saddle behind. In the arms of this dark and
handsome young man she's safe but Robert pretends
to collapse under her weight and falls backwards on
the grass, laughing and complaining. Amy falls on
top of him, Pavane skips to one side and regards the
two humans rolling around in the grass with an
expression of disdain. We are all in the grip of
uncontrollable laughter and the most dignified being
present is the horse who gives a little snort and stands
stock still.

I cast a fearful look over my shoulder and back
towards the house. I'm here to see that Amy and
Robert behave in a proper manner and rolling around
in the grass screaming with laughter does not

constitute propriety. No one's coming, thank goodness.

The scene changes. We are in the church of St Mary the Virgin and the priest is delivering his funeral sermon. He drones on and on and then I hear the words 'Lady Dudley' and 'most tragically slain'. Slain! Slain? What on earth is he talking about? Has Amy been murdered?

A piercing voice behind me screams, "God's truth! Who is this idiot? Do I have to sit here and listen to such nonsense? Will no one remove this foolish man from my presence?"

I turn around and there behind me are Robert and Elizabeth, he looking very embarrassed and she flaming with anger. What are they doing here? They weren't supposed to be among the mourners.

The scene changes and I'm sitting in the hall of the little farmhouse that Owain and I own. Over the fireplace is a portrait that I've never seen before. Owain is sitting and staring into the fire and I am looking at the painting. It depicts a man in dark clothing, a dark skinned man with a black beard, who is sitting sideways at a table, his elbow resting on it and his leg outstretched before him. The man in the painting stands and looks at me. Is it Robert? Or a Spanish gentleman? Or is it Sir Richard Verney?

"Where is she?" he shouts and then, even louder, "Where is she? Where is she?"

"Where's who?" I ask, scared out of my wits. I cast a glance at Owain who is still staring into the fire and hasn't noticed.

"Where is she?" bellows the man in the portrait, stepping out of it and onto the mantel piece. I jump to my feet, terrified.

"I don't know. Where's who? Who do you mean?"

To my horror the man in the black clothes jumps down from the mantelpiece and strides menacingly towards me.

"I don't know who you mean. Where's who?" I'm sick with fear. To my concern he now turns away from me and strides towards Owain.

"Where is she? Where is she? Here she is."

"Grandmother, grandmother look at this. Just look!"

What are my grandchildren doing in my dream. In my dream! I'm wakening, thank God, and they come rushing towards me.

"Grandmother, you were dreaming I think. You were shouting 'No, No! Go away'." They laugh.

"Look at this!" Young Philip opens his hand to show me a painted brooch.

"Philip, where did you get this? Who gave it to you?"

"A gentleman on a fine horse came riding by, grandmother. He gave me this brooch and said, "Give this to your grandmother from me. He looked very ill and when I asked him if he would like a glass of beer, he smiled and said, 'God bless you lad but no. I have to make a long journey to Kenilworth and then to take the waters in Derbyshire and I fear I will not return. You will see your grandmother gets this?' I said I would and he rode off very slowly back to his friends who were waiting for him."

"You're a good boy Philip. I think I know the man who gave you this."

I look at the pretty carved and painted brooch in my hand. It was Amy's. And there is a gillyflower for eternal love and an oak leaf intertwined. The oak leaf is a joke as the Latin for oak is quercus robur and Amy always said that stood for Robert, the English oak on whom she could always depend.

What Happened to Everyone in Our Story?

Sir Anthony Forster – bought Cumnor Place a year after Amy's death and lived there with his wife until he died, obviously unafraid of any ghosts that may inhabit the old house. After his death the Place stood unoccupied or was occasionally occupied by farmers who never stayed for long. It gradually fell into disrepair. Then Sir Walter Scott wrote his novel **Kenilworth** and interest in Cumnor was revived as tourists flocked to the area .... but it was too late since the Earl of Abingdon, who now owned the Place, had demolished it a few years earlier! It was said that he was ready to hang himself for losing the opportunity of a lucrative source of income!

Sir Richard Verney – died claiming that all the hounds of hell were after him according to the gossip of the time, and this was taken as a sure sign of his guilt by the gullible public. This 'information' was published in a libellous pamphlet, Leicester's Commonwealth, in 1583, probably instigated by Dudley's Catholic opponents. Robert Dudley was by this time a determined Puritan and follower of the teachings of Calvin.

John Appleyard – Amy's half brother who together with her illegitimate brother, Arthur Robsart, had been called by Robert Dudley to Cumnor Place to assist in the inquiry into her death – later called the inquest jury's findings into question and thought that his sister had been murdered. He was in dispute with Robert Dudley at the time over money matters. After spending a month in the notorious Fleet prison, he claimed that he had read the jury's finding and was now satisfied.

William Cecil – later Lord Burleigh, did not resign as he had threatened and continued to be Elizabeth's first minister until he died. Once the threat of a marriage between the Queen and Dudley was over, the two men respected each other and worked well together with no apparent animosity.

Sir Henry Sidney and Mary Sidney, Robert's sister – spent much of their life out of each other's company due to Henry's commission in Ireland although they remained married. Mary had suffered from smallpox, contracted while she was nursing Elizabeth through the same disease; this left her horribly disfigured and some said that she wore a mask to hide her face and that her husband found it hard to look at her. They both died in 1586.

Sir Philip Sidney – son of Henry and Mary, named after Philip II of Spain, Queen Mary's husband – had a distinguished career in the service of Queen Elizabeth and was a writer and poet like his mother. He was the apple of his uncle Robert's eye but was killed while serving with him in the Low Countries. Philip was only thirty two and Robert was devastated by his nephew's death which was tragically in the same year Philip's parents died.

Sir Robert Dudley, Earl of Leicester – waited for the Queen for many years after Amy's death. She made him Earl of Leicester in, what many saw, as an attempt to ennoble him and befit him for marriage to her. But Elizabeth realised that such a marriage would divide her kingdom and possibly lose her the crown. Robert had an illegitimate son whom he brought up in a way befitting the son of a nobleman and even allowed him to spend time with his natural mother, a very 'modern' arrangement. He later secretly married another woman, Lettice Knollys, a young, good looking and widowed lady-in-waiting at Elizabeth's court. Elizabeth was furious, banished Lettice from court and never forgave her. It seemed that Robert and Lettice were very happy, bringing up her four children from her previous marriage as their own and then having the son and heir that Robert Dudley so longed for. But their joy was short lived. Robert's beloved 'noble Imp' died aged three in 1584.

Robert was by Elizabeth's side during the crisis of the Armada and stage managed her appearance at Tilbury when, riding a magnificent prancing horse, she famously addressed her troops. This was his last duty.

Two months later Robert was passing through Oxford, on his way to Kenilworth Castle, a gift from the Queen, when he died. He had just written to Elizabeth, the letter of a friend writing to another friend, and had intended to take the waters in Buxton with the hope of easing his painful, crippling condition.

Lettice married again after Robert's death – one Christopher Blount, son of Cousin Thomas Blount! But when she died she asked to be buried in the same tomb as Robert, whom she described as the best and kindest of husbands.

The Duke of Norfolk – Robert's old enemy, who once claimed that he would hit Robert in the face with his racquet after the Queen lovingly wiped the sweat from her favourite's brow during their tennis match, was executed for treason in 1572.

Elizabeth I – never married and became known as the Virgin Queen. Two years after Amy's death she contracted small pox which, she knew, may lead to her death. Small pox was a disfiguring disease but such was the strength of Elizabeth and Robert's friendship that she wanted him at her bedside, where he remained throughout her illness. She had appointed Robert to govern in the interim period should she die. She later described him as her 'little dog', never far away from his mistress as everyone at court knew. This was not what Robert wished to hear and eventually, after their love affair, he began to re-evaluate his life, leading to his decision to marry Lettice Knollys.

Throughout Elizabeth's reign England was in the grip of a 'mini ice age', sixty years of severely cold winters and rainy summers. Towards the end three consecutive failed harvests meant that the majority of the poor people were dying of starvation. People were ready for a change just as they had been at the end of Mary's reign when the bad summers and poor harvests were just beginning. When Elizabeth died, a letter from Robert, written a few days before his death, was found in a box at her bedside; it was wrapped in ribbon and on the outside Elizabeth had written 'His last letter'.

Ironically Elizabeth died in 1603 at the Palace of Richmond, otherwise known as 'Sheen', where Amy and Robert had celebrated their wedding more than fifty years earlier.

Katherine Grey and Ned, Earl of Hertford – Their love affair ended in tragedy. Ned's sister Jane Seymour (named after her famous royal aunt) died at the tragically young age of nineteen and so the only witness to their wedding was lost, the priest being by then untraceable. Katherine was pregnant but still their marriage had to be hidden from the Queen and, to Katherine's misery, her young husband was sent on a diplomatic mission to Paris. She had no one to help her or to confide in. But the pregnancy could not be hidden for long and, when Elizabeth found out, she suspected that the marriage of Katherine and Ned had been a plot against her. Katherine was put in the Tower as was Ned, after being recalled from France. Here the warders allowed them to see each other and Katherine became pregnant again. Elizabeth, incensed with rage, split up the whole family, declaring their two sons to be illegitimate. Heartbroken at the separation from her husband and older son, Katherine, it was said, starved herself to death. Ned outlived both his sons and lived into his eighties. Ironically Ned and Katherine's descendants had a greater claim to the throne than did James I (James Stuart, son of Mary Queen of Scots) whom Elizabeth named as her successor but who should have been debarred from the succession under the terms of Henry VIII's will. Our present royal family is descended from the Stuarts.

Owain and Kat, Amy's companion – were fictional characters; that is to say they did not exist in real life. But among the ten or so servants that Amy had with her at Cumnor Place surely she deserved to have a 'Kat' to speak for her!

In our story they lived happily ever after like a prince and princess in one of Owain's folk stories.

And apologies to the Spanish Ambassador, **Bishop de la Quadra,** who was a real person and obviously enjoyed spreading the gossip about Milord Robert, whom he disliked, and Elizabeth, whom he later described as a 'baggage'. He was never documented as being involved in any plot against Robert ..... as far as we know ..... The Ambassador was finally dismissed and sent home in disgrace by Elizabeth after one of the Spaniards claimed that his master had spread the rumour that the Queen and Robert had secretly married! Presumably he did this to undermine Elizabeth and stir up trouble against her.

The Manner of Amy's Death is primarily a work of fiction fleshed out on a skeleton of fact.

The Real Story – How *Did* Amy Die?

Because of Amy's strange behaviour on the day of her death, Thomas Blount, writing to Robert, seemed to think that suicide was a possibility – not that he was willing to put such scandalous thoughts in writing. It would have constituted a disgrace for Robert if Amy had put her soul in peril by committing self murder. He simply hinted at dark things, regarding Amy's state of mind, that he wished to discuss with his master in private but which he could not set down in a letter.

Amy was a devout young woman who was seen on her knees praying for deliverance – but from what? This has been the subject of much discussion. Perhaps it was because of Robert's reportedly scandalous behaviour with Elizabeth or perhaps it was because she was seriously ill. But would this have led to the mortal sin of suicide? A more sinister possibility is that she was praying fearfully to be spared from being murdered.

Was she in a frame of mind to commit suicide? Only fifteen days previous to her death, she had written an upbeat letter to her tailor, William Edney of London, asking that he alter the neckline of one of her dresses so that it was like one that he had made for her some time earlier. And Robert was himself still sending her the sort of pretty 'accessories' that she liked so much, embroidered slippers and hoods. So Amy was still interested in her appearance. The fact that she asked for the dress to be altered as a matter of some urgency has led to speculation that she was expecting to meet someone, possibly her husband, in the very near future. As far as we know though, there was no letter purporting to be from Robert or anyone else. This was pure speculation on my part!

We should consider that, if suicide had been her intention, Amy could have chosen other, more certain, ways of killing herself rather than throwing herself down a short flight of stairs – an upstairs window, for example, or drowning in the pond or even taking poison in the form of herbs. Remember that she had suffered a dread of being harmed by poison to such an extent that it had been court gossip a year earlier, so it would seem that she had a strong sense of self preservation and was not suicidally inclined.

So was Amy murdered? Amy had previously suspected an attempt on her life by poison so this would seem to be a distinct possibility …. only …. it was common at the time for gentlemen or gentlewomen to suspect they were being poisoned whenever they suffered a stomach upset! Given the level of hygiene in Elizabethan England or the lack of knowledge concerning the safe preservation of food or indeed the use of potentially poisonous herbs, plucked from the field by the kitchen boy to disguise the taste of meat that was past its use-by date, it was hardly surprising that enteritis was a common illness. So it is possible that Amy had simply eaten something that disagreed with her and that the members of the court, jealous of Robert's place in the Queen's affections, had exaggerated Amy's fears by gossiping of attempted murder.

In many ways Robert's shock and horror when he heard the news of Amy's death and realised how he would be implicated as a murderer tends to eliminate him as a suspect. Cecil too, while fearing the increasing influence of Robert Dudley with the Queen, would have realised that any clumsy murder plot would also implicate Elizabeth, to whose service he was devoted. And if this was a murder, it was certainly performed in a clumsy way – two blows to the head and a broken neck. Not very subtle!

So this only leads to the possibility of an accident. Or does it? Would a person falling down a short flight of steps succeed in knocking two holes in their head, one two inches deep, and in breaking their neck (and, it is assumed, spinal cord) as well? It has been suggested that the 'maladie of the breast', referred to by the Spanish ambassador in his dispatches, could have been breast cancer and that, had the disease metastasised, it could have spread to the bones of the spine, resulting in Amy's neck breaking very easily when she banged her head in the fall downstairs. This would have meant that Amy was suffering from breast cancer for some years before she died, still aged only twenty eight. Yet breast cancer is, according to the Macmillan web site, very rare in women under thirty five.

What's more, Amy had travelled from Lincoln to Hertfordshire, Hertfordshire to London, London to Essex or Sussex, then to Warwickshire and on to Oxfordshire in the two years before she died, considerable journeys for a sick woman especially when we remember that she would have travelled either by horse or in a litter, a type of cart which had no springs or any kind of suspension - coach springs had not been invented in Amy's lifetime. These would have been very tedious, uncomfortable and tiring journeys for an invalid.

And would a woman who was in the terminal stages of breast cancer have taken such an interest in clothing and fashion?

It seems to me that Amy's 'maladie of the breast' was a common complaint in Elizabethan times, 'sorenes of the breast' or mastitis, a very painful condition which most women suffer in silence. This condition can occur after a stillbirth or late miscarriage when the milk glands in the breast become blocked due to the fact that there is no baby to feed. Had Amy suffered from such a condition then Robert would certainly have known about it and it may have inhibited any physical relations between them on the few occasions when Robert's work at court enabled them to live together as man and wife, thus also explaining why there were no living children and why Robert felt entitled to tell others (have a little grumble maybe) about his wife's condition. We do not know whether they had any sort of personal tragedy such as a miscarriage but such events were quite unremarkable at a time when infant mortality was common as indeed was the mortality of the mother.

Given that Amy did not have tumours in the bones of her neck, it would seem that her injuries from such a short fall were severe. Sadly the coroner's report does not say where the head injuries were located nor whether there was prolific bleeding from the site of injury. If, as the report says, the depth of one of the injuries was indeed that of two thumbs (or inches) there must have been copious amounts of blood at the site of her death. Yet nothing was reported. Indeed it was later stated that her bonnet was still in place upon her head when she was found. This may or may not be true but a two inch gaping wound must surely have meant that some sharp object had penetrated both the flesh and bone of her skull. Again it is a great pity that the building was demolished two hundred years ago and that the scene of her death cannot be re-examined.

For Amy to suffer a deep head wound which penetrated the skull she must have encountered a protruding object on the way down.

But then where was the blood? Or had someone already 'tidied' up the body, mopped up the mess and placed a clean bonnet on Amy's head? Had Amy, indeed, been attacked in another part of Cumnor Place, in the garden maybe, and her body placed at the foot of the stairs in a clumsy attempt to make her death seem like an accident? This brings us back to the same question.

Was Amy murdered?

One last thought. Since the recent discovery of the coroner's report, emphasis has been placed on the use of the word 'dyntes' or dints to describe Amy's head injuries and this has been taken to imply that they were sustained in a violent way. However this word was still used in the North of England as little as fifty years ago to mean an indentation. A metal kitchen utensil would be described as 'dinted' if it had been bashed in a little by rough usage. So when the coroner described Amy's head as having two dints, one to the depth of two thumbs, could he have meant that the indentation in her skull was two thumbs *across,* especially if the injury was on the back of her head – a common site of impact for accidental falls down stairs? In other words, could Amy's death have been an accident after all?

Author's note: If there had been magazines such as 'OK!' and 'Hello!' in Elizabethan times, the characters in our story would have featured every week on the front pages. They were the glamorous and wealthy of their age; they were, for the most part, young and sometimes behaved scandalously, living life to the full and participating in life threatening sports and activities. If ever anyone had a 'walk on the wild side', it was Elizabeth and her Master of the Horse, Robert Dudley, tall, rugged, darkly handsome and athletic, the 'Daniel Craig' of his day. He drank, gambled on anything, played cards and tennis with his male companions, got into fights, creating mayhem at times with his gang of thuggish retainers, trained horses, rode and hunted better than any other man - and borrowed large amounts of money to finance his lavish lifestyle. The young Queen, herself a better rider than most of her courtiers, was besotted with him.

There was only one problem; Robert Dudley was married.

The well-to-do Elizabethans were not altogether unlike us. They enjoyed good food, roast meat, meat pies, fish and sweet desserts. They drank copious amounts of wine, beer and ale. They loved fine clothes and liked to be seen in public dressed to kill in furs, velvet and satin. They built impressive houses and went heavily into debt to fund these luxuries, just as we today are prepared to use our credit cards to have the lifestyle we want, whether we can afford it all or not!

For the poor it was a different matter. A mini Ice Age in the second half of the sixteenth century, from 1550 to 1610 approximately, caused widespread misery, malnutrition and starvation. For these people stories of the excesses at court must have provided a degree of escapism from their own miserable lives.

The tales filtered down from above. Elizabethan gentlewomen and the Queen's ladies-in-waiting at court had little to do but gossip; indeed they referred to their best friends as their 'good gossips'. The women's chambers must have resembled the dormitories of a girls' boarding school with teenagers and young women sitting up late at night, sharing each other's bed to keep warm and talking about the latest scandal. One Elizabethan gentleman, describing such groups of women living together in royal palaces without the benefit of garderobes emptying to the outside, thought the smell from the shared 'close-stool' (privy) would be so offensive that it was a complete turn-off for any amorously inclined gentleman who entered their chambers! But even this did not deter those courtiers bent on a little illicit sex on the side.

Queen Elizabeth, however, was so particular about her personal cleanliness that she had a bath once a month, 'even when she didn't need to'!

High ranking servants often brought news of the goings on in other parts of the royal court; and so the gossip percolated downwards until it reached the men and women in the street. Gossiping was one of the main forms of entertainment for everyone.

The rich were not so different from us in matters of love either. There was marital unfaithfulness, and divorce was not uncommon, although there had to be

250

a good reason. Secret, passionate assignations took place in bedchambers and there were resulting pregnancies that women tried to hide by letting out the laces of their gowns. But, of course, such things could not be hidden for long. Members of the aristocracy who married without the permission of the Queen risked imprisonment in the Tower – or worse! But even this did not stop those who had 'the hots' for each other marrying in private so that any resulting children would not be illegitimate. From then onwards it would have been relatively easy to escape from the court for a few moments of satisfying passion. Elizabethan women usually wore no underwear other than a long washable linen shift which doubled as a nightdress!

There is however no proof that Elizabeth and Robert's affair went any further than a longing, a closeness and outrageous displays of affection. On the other hand neither was there proof that they did not have a sexual relationship. No one knows. Elizabeth never tried to hide her love for him and, at first, rather seemed to revel in the notoriety it caused. She called him her eyes, 'OO' in written correspondence. As the eyes were the window to the soul we may say today that he was her 'soul-mate'.

However it would be wrong to suggest that life was one long party. The Elizabethans worked hard and played hard; they took their responsibilities and duties seriously. For women it was a new age of intellectual freedom and the daughters of the wealthy were educated more and more to the same standards as their brothers. Elizabeth herself, Lady Jane Grey, Katherine Parr, Anne Askew and Bess of Hardwick were just some of the educated and free thinking women of the time. Anne Askew was tortured and executed by Henry VIII for her unwavering stance on religious reform while Bess became a fabulously wealthy and astute business woman.

Into this vipers' nest of strong, sometimes reckless, women and ambitious, greedy men steps a gentleman farmer's daughter from Norfolk, Amy Robsart.

Little is known of Amy's life so I have put her into situations where she may, or may not, have been involved …. Lady Jane Grey's brief reign, for example. It is, however, entirely possible that Amy interacted with all the rich and famous of the time for she was married to Robert Dudley, the son of the most influential nobleman of them all, the Duke of Northumberland. And this, ultimately, led to her downfall.

History is fun! If you have enjoyed this fictional account of a four hundred and fifty year old murder mystery, you may wish to read the non-fiction secondary sources for this book. But remember that true historians go back to primary sources as well, national archives, manuscripts and documents preserved in castles, university archives and the British Library, where there must be many documents relating to mysterious and important historical events still waiting to be discovered. Only recently has the Coroner's Report into Amy's death been found in the National Archives at Kew, under the section for October 1561. Previously, when historians searched for this document, they naturally assumed it would be filed alongside those documents relating to autumn 1560 and hence it was assumed to be lost. This discovery cast a whole new light on the mystery of Amy Robsart's death.

Non fiction Sources for The Manner of Amy's Death

De Lisle, Leanda, The Sisters Who Would be Queen (HarperPress, 2008)

Fraser, Antonia, Mary Queen of Scots (World Books, 1969)

Jones, Gwyn and Jones, Thomas (translators), The Mabinogion (Everyman, 1949)

Lipscomb, Suzannah, A Visitor's Companion to Tudor England (Ebury Press, 2012)

Rowse, A. L., The Elizabethan Renaissance, The Life of the Society (Macmillan, 1971)

X Skidmore, Chris , Death and The Virgin (Phoenix, 2011) _HAVE THIS ONE_

Starkey, David, Elizabeth (Vintage, 2001)

253

Whitelock, Anna, Mary Tudor (Bloomsbury, 2009)

19016815R00141

Printed in Great Britain
by Amazon